Holy Rollers

HOLY ROLLERS

A NOVEL

JAMES WALLACE

www.mascotbooks.com

Holy Rollers

For more information, please contact:
Mascot Books
620 Herndon Parkway, Suite 320
Herndon, VA 20170
info@mascotbooks.com

Library of Congress Control Number: 2020908076

CPSIA Code: PRV0820A
ISBN-13: 978-1-64543-488-7

Printed in the United States

Author's Note: This is a work of fiction. The characters, locations, and events herein portrayed are products of the author's imagination. Any resemblance to real people, living or dead, or to any factual events is merely coincidental. Some of the information, particularly about clinical psychology, has some basis in reality but is not intended to apply to actual diagnosis or practice. Elements of golf psychology may have value, but only if those tips match the perceptions and practices of the golfing reader. The aikido principles, which have practical implications, and the arts of self-defense, applicable only after extensive training, stem from the personal experience of the author.

"If I had to have a name for the church I would belong to, it would be something like this: the Déjà Vu Congregation of Ex-Catholic, Geo-Natural, Afro-Oceanic, Aboriginal Gypsies."

—Jimmy Buffett

"You have to accept whatever comes and the only important thing is that you meet it with courage and with the best you have to give."

—Eleanor Roosevelt

"The ultimate measure of a man is not where he stands in moments of comfort and convenience, but where he stands at times of challenge and controversy."

—Martin Luther King, Jr.

I

SHOTS

HOLY SMOKES! Wayne Windham just hit one 320 yards down the middle and expects the golf pro to help him do so consistently. Sure, he's 6'4", with enough bulk and power to hit a golf ball into orbit. But he's about as well coordinated as an inebriated, airsick guy with a pre-existing neuromuscular condition. Wayne wore a purple shirt with pink swirls that day, clashing with his strawberry blond hair, but the rest of his golfing attire—khaki shorts and beige socks with black shoes—was pretty stylish.

"Wow! That's it! That's what I want to do every time. I'm on my way to scratch golf, aren't I, Max?"

The pro thought that the big oaf should scratch "scratch golf" from his fantasies.

"That sure is the way to powder it, Wayne. You stayed steady over the ball, kept your eyes level, and finished on balance."

"So, why can't I do that every time?" His whiney, childish voice mismatched his large stature and mature appearance. Wayne's oval face fit in with his tall body. His red nose reflected either insufficient sunscreen use while on the golf course, or somewhat excessive alcohol intake when off the links.

"Why do some geese try to endure our frigid winter on the local lake?"

"Huh? Max, are you okay?" Wayne looked at his teacher with one blond eyebrow raised.

Max shrugged. "What I mean, Wayne, is that the answer is elusive. You hit some great shots. You practice regularly. You have an insight into a 'key thought,' which you expect to work for you every time. But then you go out and scatter the ball all over the course again. Let's take one step at a time. Hit a few more without further analyzing that great shot you just smacked. Just stay on balance and let the swing propel the ball toward your target."

Max wondered if he was really cut out to be a teaching pro. Sometimes he confused *himself* so much that there was no way that he could be imparting effective instruction to his pupils. Well, that's golf. And was he ever going to be able to cut the mustard at tournament golf? He'd been playing for, let's see—he started with Dad when he was five, so it'd been twenty-four years of trying to master this silly game. And here he was: Assistant Professional at Rolling Greens Golf Club in Ebbinflo, New York, second in command to a guy who breaks eighty only on good days, hoping himself to be able to follow up his occasional sixty-eight with a welcome sixty-seven instead of the inevitable seventy-nine. Sex addicts are enmeshed with erotica; Max was a golf addict who's entangled in erratica.

"Aw, Max, that's four wild shots in a row after those two good ones. How can I get more consistent?"

He's asking me? thought Max. He'd taken inconsistency to the level of an art form, and Wayne wanted *him* to come up with a remedy?

"Uh, Wayne, let's lay off the driver for a few swings. Here, stroke a few five-irons out there." *And try not to dig any more of those trenches in our practice tee turf,* he thought.

The sound of sirens penetrated their awareness and intensified in volume. Max didn't see any smoke in the vicinity, and hadn't heard any squealing brakes or sounds of an auto crash.

"Holey divot, Wayne!" That trench must be nine inches long and an inch thick. "Remember, take it back low and slow. Swing *through* the ball, not *at* it."

Golly, a police car just turned into the parking lot. Holy cow—here come an ambulance and another cop.

"Wayne, I can't help but wonder what's cookin' at the clubhouse. Let's cut it short today, and I'll owe you an extra ten minutes next week."

Wayne, however, had just whacked a five-iron shot two hundred yards down the middle after scuffing one thirty yards along the ground, and begged for Max's analysis.

By the time Max arrived at the clubhouse, the scene was truly troubling. Paramedics were just moving Pastor Puttnam toward their ambulance, and he looked bad. Blood, some wet and some dry, stained his maroon golf shirt into an even darker color than it had been when Max saw him tee off that morning. And the ooze from his head, down his neck, and into his collar was downright grisly. The paramedics hastily covered the victim with a sheet.

Max shuddered before asking no one in particular, "What happened? How did he get hurt?" He then made eye contact with Larry Bogart, one of the club's resident golf fanatics.

"A golf ball! He got decked on the thirteenth fairway from God knows where." Larry was speaking more to a heather gray-suited stranger than to Max. "I ran to him as soon as I heard the grunt and saw him crumple to the turf. We all looked around but didn't see any other players on the nearby holes. Nobody came out of the woods in search of his ball. No one. Holy Jesus! Is he gonna be okay?"

The non-golfer tightened his lips into a grimace. "It looks darn serious. I fear that Pastor Puttnam may be on his way to meet his maker."

The folks standing within earshot of the conversation collectively slumped. Max took a breath and a few steps toward Larry, an average-sized guy with unruly brown hair and rounded facial features. "It happened on number thirteen? That's an odd place for a shot to come from another hole. In fact, that's the first time I've heard of one. No other hole aims even close to there. Are you sure he was hit by a golf ball, Larry?"

"It was a Surefire XD, to be exact," the thickset, middle-aged man interjected as he turned toward Max. "We found it a few feet away from the pastor. And the wound to his head . . . what with dimples and all . . . well, *someone* hit a bad shot out that way. By the way, who are you?"

"Max Azure, the Assistant Pro here." As the man scrutinized his dark brown-haired, well-tanned, six-foot-one frame, Max inferred that the guy may be more than a casual curiosity seeker.

"I'm Detective Southworth of the Ontario County Sheriff's Department. Where were you when this happened? Did you see anybody who might have hit the shot, or witnessed it?"

"I was on the practice tee over there, giving a lesson. I can't say for sure who was playing out there today, except for some of Pastor Puttnam's pals."

"And you say there's no hole near number thirteen? It's unlikely a bad shot from another hole would go out that way?"

"That hole, like others near it, has a lot of trees on either side of it. They're tall trees. I can't imagine anyone's hitting over them by accident."

"Huh." The detective looked away for a moment and then back at Max. "Do shots sometimes go through the trees?"

"Not that I'm aware of. Plenty of shots go *into* the trees but not through 'em. Those woods are dense." Max looked aside, picturing that section of the golf course.

Larry, known to his golfing buddies as "Bogey," added, "But some of the lower branches of the trees have been cut away."

"Yes," Max explained to Detective Southworth, "so players don't have to take a long time looking for their bad shots. It speeds up play. But for a shot to go through the lower part of the trees, it would have to be scuttling along the ground. It couldn't hit anyone in the head on another hole."

"Okay, guys, thanks for the information," said the cop. His broad shoulders, burly arms, and protruding paunch filled his suit to its seams as he stood more upright and prepared to move on. "Stick around, Pro. I'd like to ask you a few more questions in a little while. Mr. Bogart, would you please point out the other guys in your group today so I can talk to them?"

Max was naturally distracted a bit as he moved on toward his next lesson of the day. He glanced skyward, subvocalizing a prayer for the departed clergyman and, involuntarily, appreciating the varying textures and shades of gray of the overcast sky. As usual, he soon got back on track due to a combination of will and circumstance. He consciously reminded himself to "be Zen," in the moment, with the reassurance that his current thoughts about the tragic accident would readily resurface at a more opportune time. He decided that he would be able to compartmentalize the disturbing distraction by telephoning his buddy, Mitch, as soon as the day's duties were done. And the process of giving his next golf lesson quickly consumed all of his visual, auditory, and mental attention.

When he subsequently arrived home to his apartment, it dawned on Max that Mitch might be more upset than he about the pastor's passing. After all, Pastor Puttnam had been the Chaplain of Confluence College during the years of Mitch's tenure there. Max had never seen them golf together, but perhaps they had interacted with one another on campus. Or maybe Mitch's students had familiarized him with the chaplain. Max wanted to inform Mitch of the mishap as soon as he could.

Max kicked off his shoes and settled down before dialing Mitch. Telephone conversations felt much less rushed and more salubrious from his recliner with a cold glass of water by his side. Judging by the time, he suspected that his call would find Mitch engaged in counseling one of his kooky clients. Sure enough, Max reached his voicemail: "Thank you for calling Dr. Treasure's affirmation line. You are a good person. You carry out your positive intentions. If you are a telemarketer, you are seeking to change to a less intrusive line of work. Your friendship knows no bounds. Your message to me will be elegantly and eloquently stated. You will enjoy the time it takes to receive my return call. If this is an emergency, call 911. The following tone will be music to your ears." Beep.

"I like your new message, Mitch. It even sounds semi-professional for a change. Please try to give me a call at your earliest convenience at home tonight or to my cell while I'm at the course tomorrow morning. If I don't hear from you, I'll see you at aikido class tomorrow night."

Knowing Mitch, he might well be too busy to call. That guy was on the go every minute, nearly as much as Max. Just then, as fate would have it, Max had nowhere to be and no people to see. His cozy one-bedroom apartment felt unusually empty and forlorn. Perhaps he had not known Pastor Puttnam well, but the close-to-home death, and its attendant mystery, disturbed him. Mitch would probably hear about the tragedy himself, without needing Max's news bulletin, and would be good to consult.

If folks were aware and wary of the fatal shot of the previous day, you couldn't tell it by the number of golfers on the links the day after Pastor Puttnam's last duff. The spring day was a "10" for golf, with blue skies, gentle breezes, occasional puffs of cloud, the temperature in the low 70s, and the seasonal advent of pesky insects not yet arrived. Max suspected that those in the know played number thirteen in one or two shots more than was customary, with visions of lethal golf balls dancing in their heads. He knew that he would have felt shaky, and curious, had he found the opportunity to play the back nine that day. And the thirteenth hole is challenging enough without fatal distractions to disrupt one's ability to hit that green in regulation.

Robert Trent Jones had designed Rolling Greens several decades earlier. He didn't name her, but the moniker flowed naturally from his product. The Finger Lakes Region of New York provided him with the undulating, sloping terrain with which to make lies interesting, but it was Mr. Jones' cutting doglegs through the trees, aiming holes in many directions vis-à-vis the prevailing winds, and constructing large, multi-tiered greens that made the course's title so apropos. One of his trademarks was the inclusion of several long, wide par-4s on his golf courses—holes that defy you to reach them in two, not because of hazards but because of sheer length (and often the wind resistance or gradual uphill slope you encounter). Two of his monsters at Rolling Greens—the 450-yard ninth and the 466-yard thirteenth—were downright diabolical because of the uneven terrain between tees and greens. It was hard enough to carry a long iron to each green to hit it in two, but having to hit the shot blind—with vision of the green blocked by a rise in the fairway about ninety yards before the putting surface—made it holy heck to execute well.

Max gave his biweekly lesson to elderly Eleanor Wholesome, a pleasant lady with an eagerness to improve her game. Frankly, she didn't need him. She could already play nearly every shot straight down the fairway, and her short game was sound. Mrs. Wholesome could not hit the ball very far, but her accuracy compensated well for her lack of power. And more power was not forthcoming to her seventy-one-year-old, pleasingly plump body. Still, he couldn't knock the former club champion's desire to keep honing her skills.

Then it was time for one of Larry's tune-up sessions. Not solely for self-serving reasons, Max admired Larry's following the advice of some golf magazines by scheduling several lessons spread out over the course of the season. Their periodic sessions on the practice tee helped him to set goals for which to shoot, made sure that no glitches had crept into his swing, and boosted his self-assurance for the various matches and club tournaments in which he played every year. Max felt pleased with Larry's progress and hoped that he had played at least a small part in it. His swing had held together pretty well through thick and thin. Of course, thanks to his horrendous putting, his nickname of "Bogey" would never be in jeopardy, no matter how many greens he became able to hit in regulation.

"Hey, Pro, how about a putting lesson today?" Larry asked in a chipper manner.

Holy Toledo, did Max spy an insight? Had Larry had an epiphany? And why didn't he seem more upset about his proximity to death on the course yesterday? His tortoise-shell eyeglasses framed his face well and maybe masked some of his emotional expressions.

"Sure, Bogey, that's a darn good idea," Max agreed with a quizzically furrowed brow.

Due to his incipient male pattern baldness, graying temples, glasses, and frumpy clothing, Larry looked older than his thirty-six years. He hit the ball far for a five-foot-eight guy because of his forearm strength. Whatever he did for a living and playing golf had firmed the muscles of his wrists and hands. As Max watched him stroke a dozen putts toward the general vicinity of a hole on the practice green, he saw Larry take varying lengths of time to execute each putt, move his eyes away from the ball at different times, and repeatedly shift his posture uncomfortably. No wonder he putted so inconsistently!

"Bogey, we're going to try to focus on just two goals for today: (1) establishing a consistent routine, both physical and mental, for each putt, and (2) keeping your eyes level—that is, looking steadily at the point of impact even after your putter has struck the ball."

Larry made some progress toward those goals in the following forty-five minutes. Maybe at his next lesson they would be able to tackle his putting grip, posture, stance, balance, aim, follow-through, judge of distance, break reading, and every other ingredient of good putting that he lacked.

"Say, Max, I want to ask you something. My aunt wants to set me up with a blind date, some cute little lady from her church. I always feel awkward on such occasions, and I know that you are seeing someone fairly regularly, so . . ." he paused and flashed a sheepish grin.

"So, you would like to double, Bogey?"

"Well, yes, depending on how you mean that."

They left Larry's golf scores his business and the dating situation as a "we'll see" proposition before wrapping up his lesson by hitting half a bucket of balls to the chipping green.

Max loved golf. He loved his job, albeit an imperfect one, as a golf pro. To think that he made money doing what he loved! But a job is a job and, as fatigue crept in during the course of a long day, he felt glad to head home for a respite.

"Hi, Mom. Greetings, Dad." Max visualized his gray-haired mother with her pretty though wrinkled face, and his tall but paunchy father with only wispy hair. "How's life in the Sunshine State?"

"Heating up in more ways than one, Son," quipped Dad. Max groaned inwardly. "The temperatures are rising, my golf scores are skyrocketing, and your mother's book club just started a steamy novel."

"It sounds like par for the course for you two. But the steamy novel, Mom—did you gals finally cave in to one of Mrs. Malamute's suggestions?"

"Yes," she chuckled. "She slipped it to us under the guise of a historical novel. It's called *Passionate Patterns*, and it does indeed outline the lives of some historical journalists in our country. It's the details that are, well, a little too risqué for my blood."

"Are you and the other ladies blushing embarrassedly, as you should, during your meetings?"

"Of course! Then I'm reading excerpts to your father to point out what he and I missed over the years. How are you doing up there in winter wonderland?"

"First of all, since it's April, even the frozen North has thawed out. Today was in the 70s, and the course was jammed. I need to mention that we had a crazy, and tragic, thing happen the other day."

"You followed a birdie with a quadruple bogey again?" insulted Dad.

"Well, yes, as a matter of fact. But I don't suppose your local newspaper mentioned anything about a death at Rolling Greens, did it?"

"No," they said almost simultaneously, with the levity drained from their voices.

"One of our members, Pastor Puttnam, got clocked in the head by a golf ball."

"Holy Moses! I remember him. Nice guy, lousy golfer. Ooh, that *is* tragic. Yet I'm surprised it doesn't happen more often," responded Dad.

"And I've spent years fearing it would happen to you, or that you would hit someone yourself, Max," confessed Mom.

"Well, I've just been lucky, I guess. People can and do hit some awfully wild and dangerous shots. But this one was pretty strange. It happened on a tree-lined hole where an errant shot was highly unlikely to travel. No one *ever* hits there from another hole—it happened nowhere near any other target."

"So, what are you saying? That it wasn't a golf ball? Or it wasn't an accident? Could it have been hit by another guy in the pastor's group?" queried Dad.

"It was a golf ball, all right. Accident, I suppose so; the police are apparently chalking it up as such. As for the other guys in his group, I seriously doubt that they were out to get Pastor Puttnam. Maybe another pastor and a priest didn't see eye-to-eye with him spiritually, but . . . And Larry Bogart, a local engineer and member of the church choir, had been playing with the pastor for years; they were partners."

"What about the group behind them?" asked Dad.

"Another blend of local clergy and businessmen. They were just approaching the tee when the incident happened. They saw nothing."

"You be careful out there, Son," warned Mom predictably.

"Well, we've got people wearing helmets now for any activity from biking to skateboarding, and from skiing to snowmobiling," declared Max. "Maybe golf will be next!"

Max's conversation with his parents moved through a review of their favorite local restaurants and the early bird specials there, events in the lives of his parents' friends and in the lives of the friends' children, and a reiteration of just how nice the weather is in Florida—the usual stuff of which retirees speak. Mom recounted the joys of swimming, and Max his regrets of not being able to do so with her. Then they got around to Max asking about the well-being of his siblings: older sister, Ruth, working her way through the ranks as a college professor and raising two lovely daughters in Ventura, California, and younger brother, Zeke, attending a special school for the treatment of Autism Spectrum Disorder (ASD) in Amherst, Massachusetts. They spoke lightheartedly about Zeke's good grades and positive prognosis, but Max could always detect, just beneath the surface, their lament about his not being "normal."

They gradually rounded off their conversation. Mom and Dad inquired about his tournament schedule for the season and asked if he was still actively involved in that offbeat activity, aikido.

"Why would a guy who constantly has golf clubs within reach ever need to resort to hand-to-hand self-defense?" Dad asked for the umpteenth time. They understood his explanation, Max guessed, but he sensed that their suspicion that the foreign art is too exotic would linger and resurface again and again.

II

MIX & MATCH

"MITCH AND MAX ARE A NATURAL MATCH." Thus pronounced their aikido master, Kikai Sensei, to his assistant instructor standing just within
their earshot. It was nice praise. Since aikido is an art of self-defense
that emphasizes harmony with natural forces, it was good that Sensei
perceived them to be blending well with one another.

Fortunately, Max did not let the momentary distraction interfere with
his concentration as he attacked Mitch. Whoosh! The sound of Max's
hakama—the long, flowing, black or navy culottes worn by advanced
students over their white judo uniforms—hitting the mat was soft and
unobtrusive. It beat the heck out of the sound, and feel, of his legs
thumping against the surface. Ever since he had first joined aikido class
and learned to roll, he had done so pretty well. At least, some observers
had said that he seemed round and graceful. He could usually curve
his medium-build body into a decent ball, but he often wondered if
onlookers could see the "edges" in his body and the pained expression
on his face when he occasionally landed badly. Ugh—self-fulfilling
prophecy. Think and ye shall receive. Brown-haired Mitch, as skilled as
Max, slightly taller, and built with a similar frame, had just tossed him
a couple of extra feet across the mat as though he were reading Max's
mind and testing his present capacity to fall with style.

"It's time to reverse our offense/defense roles," Max and Mitch said tacitly, with a bow to one another rather than words. As Mitch swung his arm at his head in the forty-five-degree arc that defines the *yokomenu-chi* attack, Max slid aside and slightly inward, raising and then dropping his own arms in synchrony with Mitch's intended strike to his head. After pushing lightly upon Mitch's arm in union with his assault, but carrying him just slightly beyond its intended conclusion, Max pivoted neatly beside his partner to lead him forward and upward—a little past his balance point—then downward toward the mat. *Sumi-otoshi* is an art that epitomizes the aikido way of blending with the force of an attacker; it infrequently hyperextends the elbow of one's partner a bit if done with too much vigor or inaccuracy, but it's usually a flowing and effective means of dispensing with that partner. Mitch did a nifty forward roll as a result of the throw. Aikido visually resembles judo in that its practitioners take turns attacking one another, make contact, and put the assailant down onto a tumbling mat. Aikido, however, involves more open-handed guiding of one's partner and less wrestling-like grappling.

"That was smoothly done, partner," said Mitch with a smile. He must have done a good roll. His composure also indicated that, as he had informed Max, he had not known Pastor Puttnam well enough to feel painfully distraught about his death. They had encountered one another mainly vicariously through mutual student contacts at Confluence College, so Mitch's reaction to the news had been limited to surprise and sympathetic concern.

"That throw was about as smooth as my wedge shot into the ninth green last Sunday," Max recalled.

Instinctively, Max glanced at Sensei and, as expected, he had noticed their brief conversation but not necessarily the five silent, intense minutes of training that had preceded it. As he approached, Max adroitly neutralized Mitch's attack and moved him neatly into a fall. Sensei swung at him in exactly the same way and, as too often happens, the trace of adrenaline that oozed into Max's bloodstream caused him to bump rather than blend with his teacher. A little extra muscle compensated for his clumsiness sufficiently to finish the throw. But Max was again, as in the past, left with the temptation to say, "But Sensei, I really know how to do it better than that, honest I do." It was uncanny how that nice man could make his students so nervous, probably because they respected him so much.

"Relax, Max," said Sensei. Then, as though blending with Max's thoughts, he added, "I've seen you do that more smoothly." Mitch and Max bowed to his retreating back, in keeping with dojo etiquette, after he adroitly pivoted and walked away to see other students.

Aikido resembles judo for good reason. The Japanese founder of the former, Morihei Ueshiba, incorporated what he considered the best parts of his judo training into aikido. Aikido students simulate attacks—punches, overhead and angular strikes, holds, and multiple-person assaults—in order to neutralize them with the least force necessary to do so. Mr. Ueshiba also used his lessons from karate and *kenjutsu*—the samurai art of swordsmanship—to shape the escapes, throws, cutting movements, and controlling pins of this effective, energy-efficient martial art. His devotion to the *Ōmoto-kyo* religion tempered the arts of aikido into a path of ethical, non-injurious practice.

Ever since Max and Mitch first met in this earnest yet congenial aikido club, they had appreciated one another's amicable approach to the nonviolent art of self-defense. They both tended to chat discreetly with their partners during training, mixing small talk with helpful pointers. When they were paired up or grouped for a series of throws, as they were at present, they effectively balanced a good-natured demeanor with little competitive urges to thwart the other's attempts to execute the arts at hand. When they went out after class for a brew or two that fateful Friday evening seven years earlier, and discovered that one of them was a golfer with a keen interest in sport psychology and the other was a golfing psychologist, their friendship was launched.

"Mitch, I cannot for the life of me comprehend how a guy can get whacked in the head with no one being immediately accountable for it." Ow! Max landed a bit awkwardly that time. Aikido training was fun—

one of the mainstays of his existence—but sometimes Max crunched when he got tossed onto the mat. "Several players have been hit by balls over the years, even one on number thirteen. But it's always been readily apparent who did it and from where. Most importantly, no one has ever died from such an incident at Rolling Greens."

"Did they question the groups who were playing nearby holes?" Ahh. That was a better roll. Mitch, at two inches taller than Max, was just as wiry strong. Since they had started aikido classes at about the same time, it was no surprise that he could fling Max so fluidly. "Couldn't someone have hit a wayward shot over the trees and been naïve as to its eventual landing point?"

"The police seemed to do a pretty thorough job. I was impressed by Detective Southworth, even though I resented his taking twenty minutes of my time when I couldn't possibly have known anything about the mystery shot. What gets me is that a shot from any distance—coming over the tall trees from number eleven, for instance—shouldn't have had the velocity to kill a man on the spot. At least, I don't think so. And I overheard the police mutter something about the angle of the impact that would suggest a line-drive shot—but from where?"

"However it happened," Mitch summed up, "that man will be missed. My students who knew Pastor Puttnam always spoke well of his good-spirited nature and willingness, at any time, to talk with them."

Oops! Sensei was rather lax about discipline in the dojo. He even encouraged some verbal interchange in the interest of helping partners learn techniques better. But that look! He *knew* from their expressions that Mitch and Max were discussing something unrelated.

"Okay, Mitch, strike once more," invited Max. "Ahh, that's better. That's how *yokomenuchi hiji-otoshi* should feel. Calm. Keep one-point. Contact is down." Talking to himself, in the guise of addressing someone else, always helped both focus and technique. And Sensei sensed that the brotherly duo were back on track.

Just about the time that the advanced aikido class was wrapping up for that Friday evening, a very different gathering was taking shape about seventy miles west of the dojo. Seated at a booth in a quiet little Mexican restaurant on Elmwood Avenue in Buffalo were three men. The smallest of them opened the conversation after glancing around the room to ensure that no one was within hearing range. "Two down, too many to go. You guys obviously made a clean getaway from that course in Ebbinflo."

"Yeah, Claude, clean as a whistle," said the huge companion. Frank, with a tall and heavy frame, most of it muscle, leaned back and made the fabric of his extra-large sweat suit stretch beyond its normal limit. "We nailed the dude and hightailed it out of there without a trace."

"And from what we could see," said the third man in a confident tone, "there were even more holy men playing golf at that club than we first thought."

Claude nodded approvingly. "That's good to hear, Tony. Then we can make many happy returns, especially since you found the gig to be easily done." Tony, though smaller than Frank, still loomed larger than Claude. If they had been a football team, Frank would have played the offensive line, Tony would have been a linebacker, and Claude would have been the placekicker.

"How about our other guys, Bart and Ernie, who knocked off the priest south of town?" inquired Frank.

"Same story as you—the Ninjutsky brothers had easy pickin's. It's considerate of our targets to stick together on the golf course; we get 'em out in the open and get to choose which one of the bunch we want to hit."

Tony thought out loud. "I suppose Ebbinflo remains a place to go, but we better lay low for a few days before going back for another."

"You betcha," said Claude with a satisfied smile. "Our next meeting is at Bart's place tomorrow night at eight. We'll make our plans then. For now, let's eat."

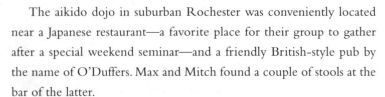

The aikido dojo in suburban Rochester was conveniently located near a Japanese restaurant—a favorite place for their group to gather after a special weekend seminar—and a friendly British-style pub by the name of O'Duffers. Max and Mitch found a couple of stools at the bar of the latter.

"Why? That's all I want to know, Mitch, is why?"

"Okay, you've got me. Why what?"

"Why can't I maintain perfect balance through each and every golf swing, just the way I can do when swinging a *bokken*?" Max ordered a pint of Bubblybrew while Mitch asked for his usual Brainmeister.

"Do you mean besides the obvious answers that a wooden sword is different than a golf club, the swing planes are totally different, and your *bokken* is intended to strike air molecules and an imaginary target while your golf club aims to propel a ball a couple of hundred yards toward a tangible and precise landing place? You already know those answers, right?"

"Well, yes, though maybe not as clearly as you just stated them. But one reason that we train aikido is to apply our learning to our everyday lives, right? And for guys like us, golf is a big application."

"Speak for yourself, golf pro."

"Oh, and you aren't a golfaholic, pal?"

Mitch gestured helplessly with his arms, shrugged, mumbled, "Well," and had a gulp of beer. Max took a sip from his mug; he had developed a taste—or at least a tolerance of the taste—for beer over the years, though it could never compete with water or juice for his thirsty affections.

Mitch redirected the subject toward a related topic. "You know what you're doing out there, Max, both on the course and on the mat. And speaking of your high levels of performance, let's schedule your guest appearances at my sport psychology course and golf team practice at the school."

"So, Dr. Shrink," Max said with mock annoyance, "you are trying to flatter me away from my pleasant immersion in self-doubt and manipulate me to do your bidding at Confluence College. Some ethical guy you are!"

"You saw right through me, Max. You might become a pretty good amateur psychologist," Mitch said with a grin. "So, how about it? Pull out your phone and check your appointment calendar."

"Not so fast, you shyster. First, I need to bounce some ideas off you."

"Such as?"

"Such as our shared goal of developing mind, body, and spirit through our aikido training. We learn to focus on key thoughts, in the dojo to keep ourselves balanced and ready to move in whatever manner is dictated by the force and direction of attack, and on the golf course to prepare our bodies to hit shots and stroke putts with repeated accuracy."

"Better said than done," kidded Mitch.

"Didn't you say something about my 'high levels of performance' a minute ago? Anyway, let me finish. Our bodies we develop not only through our golf and aikido but via cross-training. What about spirit? How are we doing in that regard?"

"What do you mean, 'we?' I attained enlightenment years ago, but you, Max, I'm afraid that you are in for a long haul."

"O Great Learned One," Max intoned while taking another sip of beer, "thank you for your wise and patient counsel. Seriously, though, the philosophical principles of aikido relate great to golf, if not everything else."

"Yes, and we could infer from the presence of so many clergy on the golf course that the game may have some spiritual overtones," interjected Mitch.

"Sure. You and I don't seem destined for a religious life, but we seem to share spiritual pursuits with the likes of Father Mulligan, Rabbi Greene, and Reverend Rollins, among others. We strive to live in the present, keep life's setbacks in perspective, let our *ki* flow through self-expression, and stay calm in adversity."

"Yes, and that is why I'd like you to visit my class and team every semester—so that you can explain all of this to a wide, impressionable audience."

"You're patronizing me again, Mitch. Okay, let's check our schedules."

As they compared dates and settled on one, dates came to mind in another context. Maybe the thought was helped along by their mutual glimpse of two samples of feminine pulchritude entering the pub and sitting across the room near the dart board. The young ladies glanced in their direction and paused only slightly before doing a double take. Mitch's broad shoulders, upright posture, and handsome dark features often evoked that response by members of the fairer sex. Max's clean-shaven face, cloaked in a masculine five o'clock shadow much of the time, likewise earned its share of female attention. His slightly oversized schnozzola, a source of teasing and self-deprecation during childhood, detracted only slightly from Max's adult appearance.

Putting female distractions aside, he switched his train of thought back on track. "You haven't answered my questions yet, Mitch. What are your views on spirituality?"

"I agree with you, Max. And, no, I'm not just kissing up to you. In the dojo, we strive to be fully present. We seek to gain an 'edge' over any potential adversary by learning to coordinate our mental and physical energies. We have a stated goal of self-victory, winning by remaining in control of our emotions and thoughts. Like the practitioners of other martial arts, and various spiritual pursuits, we want peace of mind. It may seem overly simplistic, but we move toward those goals by remaining mindful of how to unify mind and body."

"The Four Principles," Max interjected.

"Sure thing. The first, to keep one-point, means to be cognizant of the physical center of balance just below the navel. The second is to relax naturally in a controlled fashion—to stay calm and let our muscles activate themselves just the right amounts to suit any situation. Third, we want to settle down, to use rather than fight the force of gravity. We strive to feel grounded. Lastly, we let our *ki* flow by embracing the sense that our energy flows outward through our fingertips, senses, verbalizations, and personality; visual imagery aids the execution of both aikido techniques and golf shots."

"Nicely stated, Professor," Max replied. "You should teach a course in that." Mitch dipped his head, frowned slightly, and looked askance at Max through the top parts of his eyes. Max added, "Listen, if you do not patronize me, then surely I do not do so to you."

"Does my worthy explanation make me enlightened?"

"Only if you actualize it, Mitch. Only if you can live consistently in a centered, here-and-now, and effective manner. Personally, I suspect that intermittent Zen with-it-ness is the best that we can do."

"Do you suppose that reverends, rabbis, and priests feel peace of mind at all, or most, times?" asked Mitch sincerely.

"Not if they play golf!" Max retorted, revealing his own nagging sense of frustration with that splendid game. "Seriously, though, I suppose that men and women of the cloth find great reward and comfort in their lifestyles. I certainly hope that was true of poor Pastor Puttnam."

"He's still on your mind, eh?"

"It's not so much that I miss him, since I did not know him well. It's the gnawing in my gut, my nagging inability to make sense out of how he could have been killed by an anonymous golf shot, that troubles me."

"You read too many detective novels, Max. Sometimes I think that your alter ego is Sherlock Holmes, Travis McGee, and Spenser rolled into one."

Max found the number at the top of his list of recent calls. *This must be getting serious*, he thought, as he heard the ringing signal.

"Hello," said the mellifluous, feminine voice.

"Melody, I'm glad you're still up. I feared that it was a little late to call and was going to hang up after three rings."

"You caught me on the way to floss and brush. No problem, Max. I'm glad that you called."

"I wanted to talk to Mitch for a while after aikido class tonight, so I bought him a brew and, as you might guess, it stretched to two."

"Are you confessing a drinking problem to me, Max? If I'm going to accept any more dates with you, cutie, I want to know what I'm getting into."

"To paraphrase Alfred E. Neuman, 'What, you worry?' I may have bought a second one for Mitch, but I just nursed my first to quench my thirst."

"Holy moly, Max. You and your rhymes."

Max visualized the way that Melody tilted her auburn-haired head a bit to her left when she smiled. "And have I told you that no longer does Max eat Sugar Smacks for snacks?"

"Yes, well, that was my secondary concern about you. And just what do you usually munch on?" she asked with a chuckle.

"Only the best, honey: Holey Oats or Wholly Oats." He spelled them out. "I eat one on one day, and the other the next."

Her giggles made all thought of Pastor Puttnam drain from his brain for the time being.

III

MATCH-UPS

SATURDAYS WERE ALWAYS INSANELY BUSY AT MAX'S, or any, golf course. It was not so much giving lessons that consumed his time. It was helping to settle disputes about which group got to tee off next when one member of the on-deck group was late for their starting time. It was retrieving carts that had run out of power near the distant fifteenth tee. Folks were in the mood for borrowing and trying out, but not necessarily buying, clubs. A Xerox executive with a lifelong, incurable slice decided he needed lessons every Saturday because he could not stand to play another business round in which he searched the woods so often that he could not sustain a conversation with his clients. Stu Swingster, the Head Professional at Rolling Greens, had typically been too busy schmoozing with club members to help Max run their pro shop and monitor the course. College students defied the club dress code by stripping down to T-shirts or, worse, no shirts at all, and Max was the one called upon to hunt them down to warn them to look sharp. (It pained him, too, since he would love to have been able to play in a swimsuit and nothing else.) Still, no matter how hectic things became, Max usually managed to set aside an early evening each weekend for a round of golf of his own.

Max and Mitch took on Rabbi Greene and Father Mulligan that Saturday.

"I think that it is wonderful that men of your professions do not consider it sacrilegious to play golf, particularly on or near the Sabbath," Max told the clergymen on the first tee.

"If God had not intended us to golf," said the priest in the Boston Irish accent that was his birthright, "He would not have created the sport." He took the smooth practice swing of a man who had been playing golf for many years.

"And it must be clear to you why I chose to accept a position as rabbi in a Reform congregation, Max. Indeed, the Conservative or Orthodox Rabbinate would probably not look kindly upon the timing of this diversion." The bald, stocky rabbi's three-quarter swing showed a hitch in it, but he usually brought the clubhead back on line at the point of impact.

"I certainly find golf to be consistent with following a spiritual path," Max observed as he pulled on his golf glove. "For one thing, I liken the golf course to a Japanese or Zen garden. Everything is just so. The landscape is neatly manicured at all times. Water flows here and there. The greenery is lush and embellished by sand, boulders, and assorted shrubbery. Sometimes as I am playing, either alone or with guys like you, I 'stop to smell the roses,' so to speak. I look around to reflect upon the peaceful nature and beauty of the place."

"Yes, but the peace got shattered a couple of days ago when poor Pastor Puttnam got sent to the big links in the sky," said Father Mulligan. Probably distracted by the disturbing thought, he duck-hooked his drive into the trees just off the tee.

"Go ahead, Father, hit another one," Mitch said as Max and Rabbi Greene, about to say the same thing, nodded their assent.

"God bless you," invoked Father Mulligan as he teed up a second ball and stroked it down the fairway.

"I was playing behind the pastor the other day," said Rabbi Greene as he teed up his ball. "I cannot for the life of me understand where that shot came from." His practice swing was crisply on track; his swipe at the ball, however, was rushed. He still managed to slice it down into the right rough about two hundred yards in the general direction of the green.

"Well, the Good Lord giveth us the wonderful game of golf, and He taketh it away from Pastor Puttnam when He thought the time was right," Father Mulligan pontificated.

"Amen," muttered the foursome.

The fourth hole at the Golf Club of Ithaca is a lovely and challenging dogleg to the right. It's a lengthy par-4. The dense woods that line the entire fairway are obstacles enough, but the large trees that stick out at the bend and just before the green make accuracy essential. The slope of the fairway from right to left, inviting straight tee shots to leak into the rough or, worse, the forest, does not make things easier. Neither do the bunker in the left front of the green, the extreme slope left of the green, or the lightning-quick green itself.

That Monday, Father Tompkins hit one of his best drives ever on the hole. He nailed a power fade that curved around the intrusive tree and headed down the right center of the fairway. It hit the slightly slanting upslope and stopped in the middle, about 160 yards—or a six-iron away for the priest—from the center of the green. Normally, he would have helped his two playing partners look for their errant drives in the right and left woods, respectively. But Father Tompkins was distracted by his good start that day—two pars and a bogey—and eager to prepare for his second shot into the green. The pious priest never knew what hit him. Neither did his partners due to their searches for their balls in the underbrush. They heard nothing except the grunt from the center of the fairway, which they each thought at first to indicate that Father Tompkins had come upon his ball and found it in a bad lie.

This time, the police were not too quick to write off the death as accidental. An off-target shot from the third tee would need to have traveled drastically left, over or through a huge expanse of trees, to come anywhere near the clergyman's position. The fifth hole, a par-3 that runs perpendicular to number four, had nobody on it. Could the deadly shot have emanated from the forest ahead of Father Tompkins? What about from the vicinity of the horse pastures and barns that lay just beyond the woods on the right? Investigators were stumped.

She was always punctual for her Tuesday appointment with Mitch.

"Dr. Treasure, I hope you don't mind my bringing my mother along for our session today," said Haley in her sweet, polite voice.

"So, your mother has come with you today?"

"Why, yes, of course. She's sitting right there behind you."

Obligingly, Mitch glanced over his shoulder. "Oh, your mother is right here?" Haley nodded. "Well, Haley, I believe that you see your mother in the room with us, but she's not really here."

"Yes, of course she is. Right there. Don't you see her? Didn't you hear her say 'hello?'"

"Frankly, no, Haley, but that's okay. It's all right that you see and hear her. I believe that you do right now. But she's not truly here. Your mind is just playing another little trick on you."

Some therapists believe that they should empathize at all times; it is therapeutic to connect with the thoughts and feelings of your counsel-ees in order to empower them to move along paths of self-exploration toward their own healthy decision making. To dispute a client's subjective reality can undermine self-confidence and mutual trust. In most situations, Mitch agreed—that is also consistent with aikido, which teaches harmonizing with external forces as a means of redirecting them along a more desirable, non-injurious path. In Haley's case, however, Mitch diverged slightly. He empathized with her by acknowledging her hallucination and affirming her perception, but he refused to "buy into" it any further. A psychologist must remain grounded in truth and reality as much as possible. Delusions are not to be encouraged. Indeed, his strategy worked well with Haley.

"She's not really here, huh?" Haley frowned and looked down at her lap. "Sometimes my meds just don't work well enough."

"What are you taking now, Haley? Has your psychiatrist, Dr. Script, changed your meds or dosage?"

Haley, well-groomed except for disheveled blonde hair, idly scratched the little scars on her wrist. "I was starting to have too many side effects from Clozapine, so she has been switching me to Risperidone."

"Do you make that change little by little?"

"Yes, and come to think of it, maybe I forgot to take the new medication today. Oops!" Her face revealed self-criticism and forgiveness, in rapid succession. "Is that why I thought my mother had come along with me today, Dr. Treasure?"

"That could do it! Well, that would be a relief, eh? Medication is not a cure-all, but it surely has some benefit, doesn't it, Haley?"

Mitch and Haley continued to discuss medication effects, particularly their therapeutic threshold. Mitch then asked, "How do other people react when you mention that your mother is nearby, when she isn't really, or when you report seeing or hearing something that is not truly there?"

"They think I'm nuts!" exclaimed Haley with a knowing smile. "Holy mackerel, I am a little crazy, aren't I?" They shared a laugh.

"You have hallucinations. You have a biochemical condition that occasionally causes your brain to visualize or hear things that are not real. But crazy? You're sane enough to realize what is happening. You are self-aware of many of the false sightings as they arise, right?" Haley nodded, though hesitantly enough to indicate that she could not always distinguish reality from fantasy. "So, Haley, you cannot *always* tell truth from fiction, eh?" She nodded more emphatically. "Then we have something worthwhile on which to work today." Mitch and Haley proceeded to discuss the specifics of her hallucinations—their content, usual settings, stimuli that trigger them, and ways to raise self-awareness of what is real or not.

"Dr. Treasure, I usually don't say this to anyone, but I feel scared when I see my mother and then realize that she is not really there," confided

Haley. "I don't know if I'm more afraid that she could really be present, or that I could be imagining things out of my control."

He responded slowly and clearly, "That can be distressing." Mitch's simple affirmation caused Haley to sigh with the relief of feeling understood.

Next, Mitch shifted his focus to Haley's psychosocial skills training. He had her practice self-talk to question herself about the validity of her hallucinations and to resist the urge to blurt out her misperceptions to strangers. He assigned her homework: "When you see or hear something odd, that you suspect is not real, admit your suspicion to yourself and tell yourself to wait before sharing it with others. Try this five or six times before next week." He then reiterated previous advice about healthy diet and exercise before sending Haley on her way.

The telephone rang. "Hello. Dr. Treasure . . . Hi, Priscilla, I'm glad you called . . . Yes, I got your messages here at the office, but you know that I often run over in my sessions, have to take notes, and don't have time to call you back right away . . . Yes, I remember that we are going to the opera in Rochester tonight . . . We have to leave that early? Holy health, that *is* cutting it close to my last session of the day . . . All right, all right, I'll pick you up by 6:15 by hook or by crook . . ."

Mitch checked the waiting room, greeted his next clients, but asked them to wait a minute while he grabbed another phone call.

"You busy?" Max asked.

"To the max, Max."

"I'd like to toss some ideas around with you. The police just called and—"

"How about first thing in the morning? Is that soon enough? I've got a date with Priscilla right after these clients, and you know how she is."

"Yes, it can wait. It's just more about Pastor Puttnam, and nothing can bring him back at this point. Call me."

Mitch met a married couple who had decided that they should seek help with their increasingly tenuous relationship. Barry and Beth had been married for five years after having dated for a little over two years. In their early thirties now, they were the proud parents of a son, three, and a recently-born daughter. The partners smiled agreeably and gave Mitch an initial impression of being well adjusted and intelligent. Their body language, however, betrayed the tensions they were feeling.

Asked to sit on Mitch's comfortable chairs, obliquely angled toward one another, Barry had his extended legs crossed and his hands clasped in his lap. Beth was more oriented toward Mitch than her husband, with her arms crossed and her gaze avoidant of Barry's eyes.

Mitch gathered demographic and insurance data. The couple described their health as unremarkable and their careers—he a local dentist, she an administrative assistant at Confluence College—proceeding nicely. Asked their reason for seeing Mitch, they glanced at one another and adjusted their postures nervously. Spillage followed. Beth had sublimated any romantic yearnings into parenting. Barry loved his children dearly but began to feel jealous of the attention they drew from Beth. He felt compelled to stray toward more evenings out with the guys. She wanted to bring the kids more frequently to the home of her parents two hours away. Their parenting philosophies and practices clashed. So did some of their underlying values and political views. Neither trusted the other.

Mitch gave each spouse an uninterrupted chance to express what he/she expected of the other, from mundane sharing of household responsibilities to more intimate emotional nurturance. Heat began to build as their unfulfilled desires, whether shared or disparate, came to light. Mitch needed to squelch a few expressions of profane language by the lovers. Fortunately, the mood softened as the pair improved their communication with the aid of Mitch's structured format. Having typed as they spoke, Mitch printed a copy of the expectations for Beth and Barry to take home to ponder and discuss. He felt pleased when he glanced out his window to see them conversing amicably beside their car in his parking area.

"Howdy, pardner," were the drawled words that greeted Max by telephone at the pro shop early the next morning.

"Hey, Mitch. How was your date with the legal eagle, pretty Priscilla? What did you go do together?"

"She dragged me, I mean, we went to the opera at the Eastman Theatre."

"Oooh, high-brow stuff. Was it fun? Did you understand or at least like it?"

"I respected it. It takes guts, talent, and a lot of breath control to sing like that. Even though I could hardly follow the plot, I could tell that there was a lot of it; the performers have a complex show to memorize."

"Pretty boring, huh?"

"I didn't say that! I will admit, however, that I hope not to attend another operatic performance for a month or two, or five, or twenty. Say, what did the police want with you, Max? Have they finally recognized your masquerading as a golf pro as a crime?"

"No, my students have not turned me in, at least not yet. Detective Southworth did his homework and found that another clergyman, south of Buffalo, had been killed recently. He called me after a police officer in Ithaca made a similar computer search in connection with the death of yet another, a priest named Father Tompkins, on Monday and contacted him for details about the death at Rolling Greens."

"Holy guacamole! It sounds like serial killings, or God is sending a serious message about the game that we revere."

"Yes, and Detective Southworth, who may well be a God-fearing man, leans toward the former possibility."

"And why is he letting you in on this? Are you a suspect? What does he want from you?"

"A suspect? Yeah, right! He said that the police want to know more about golf and, specifically, how accurately a shot can be struck."

Mitch quipped, "Did you tell him about your knack for hitting shots precisely on target once or twice per month?"

"Actually, Mitch, I told him how adept you are at hitting shots out of the woods, owing, of course, to your habit of hitting crooked tee shots."

"Touché!"

"I told him the truth as I see it—that even the touring pros, for all their skill, would find it nearly impossible to hit a target as small as a human head from any sizeable distance. There have been some renowned trick-shot artists—Joe Kirkwood and Paul Hahn in the past, Wesley and George Bryan nowadays—who seemed able to pull some fancy and precise shots out of their bags, but even guys like that would be unlikely to hit a head at fifty paces."

"All in all," observed Mitch, "it sounds as though Pastor Puttnam's mishap deserved the doubt and sense of mystery you felt about it at the time."

"Yes, I feel validated, Doc. But the mystery gnaws at me." Max thought about his penchant for reading detective and suspense novels. He had often been praised by teachers, as well, for the deductive reasoning skills that he had demonstrated in school.

"That's business for the police, not a golf pro," advised Mitch.

"Yes, but it struck too close to home. And what if . . . you know . . . it could happen again."

"And the police have no leads?"

"No, except that the other deaths occurred in places that, like our own number thirteen, were unlikely to have such shots happen. I've played Ithaca a few times before, and it happened on a tree-lined hole on which shots never cross over from other holes."

"Let the good doctor help you get your mind off this, Max. Tell Dr. Treasure your pleasure: Go out after aikido class tonight, or play nine holes tomorrow evening?"

Max chose both.

IV

INTERACTIONS

MELODY TELEPHONED MAX EARLY THAT THURSDAY EVENING. She reached his voicemail and heard him sing his tortured rendition of "My Bonnie Lies Over the Ocean":

"The reason my phone's not still ringing
Is I have my voice here on tape,
And if you can stand my bad singing,
You'll have your chance soon to go ape.
So please sing back, sing back,
Act the buffoon and croon loony tune,
And I'll ring back, ring back,
I'll call you back very soon."

As fate would have it, Max was singing in the shower when she called. Luckily, he checked his cell phone soon after he emerged from the bathroom. Melody's message started with a pause as she collected herself from her amusement—or shock. Then she said, "That's terrible, Max! Truly awful," she lectured, with a telltale trace of mirth in her tone. "Um. Well, anyway, I'm not feeling melodious enough right now to sing a reply, but please give me a call about tonight. Maybe I should sing a tricky greeting onto my voicemail. Bye."

Now not knowing what clothing to don for fear that she had called to cancel their date, Max called her back immediately.

"Hello."

"Miss Melody Klef, please," Max said in a slightly high-pitched, Irish accent.

"Yes, speaking."

"This is Clem Blarney of the Helioray Sunspot Company, and I'm calling to inquire—"

"Max, is that you?" she interrupted.

"Either you're getting good at recognizing my voice, or I'm losing my touch."

"Both, you weirdo," she cajoled.

"You rang? You called simply to tell me how excited you feel about getting together with me this evening?"

"Yes, I called. Excited? Gee, I don't know about that. You're a pretty boring guy. But the reason I called is to ask how dressy the restaurant is. Like, should I dress as if going to work, as a broadcast journalist, or going for a workout?"

"Chez Burrito offers casual ambience, I assure you. It's not just a taco joint, but neither is it a gourmet restaurant. Your usual well-groomed self should be just fine."

"And you'll pick me up at 7:00?"

"Yes. That'll give us time to swing by the Helioray Sunspot Company so I can give that jokester, Clem, a piece of my mind."

If Max could manage to amuse himself at times, that was good. If he could provoke a giggle from Melody, that's better.

The following evening, Friday, Max and Mitch were in the dressing room preparing for the evening's aikido class when the latter asked, "Have you ever met Melody's sister, Harmony?"

Max answered, "I could make beautiful music with either one of them." Mitch responded with a grin and a groan. Max continued, "Well, no, I've never met Harmony. Melody says that they are very similar, in personality as well as looks, but I have no firsthand knowledge of that."

"Maybe Harmony is as pretty and nice as her sister," said Mitch wistfully.

"I'm just glad that I'm getting to know Melody pretty well; the way we talk to each other, her mannerisms . . ." He trailed off as he worked to tie the straps of his *hakama*. "Of course, Harmony is involved with some guy and probably too busy seeing him to cross paths with me. And speaking of love life," Max adroitly redirected the subject, "how are things going with Priscilla?"

"Ah, sweet Priscilla. She acts a little prissy sometimes—"

"That comes with the territory, doesn't it?"

"—But we seem pretty happy with one another."

"You sound less than convincing," Max observed.

"Hey, buddy, I'm the psychologist around here, remember?" Mitch chided playfully. They headed toward the doorway and bowed their way onto the aikido mat.

After Sensei opened the class with the traditional bows and mutual greeting, "*Onegaishimasu*," which means "please teach me," he departed somewhat from the usual class routine. Instead of ending instruction with *bokken* practice, he started by having the students make one hundred cuts with the wooden sword. Then he ventured radically from the martial arts tradition of Japan, the land of thoroughly right-handed *samurai*. He had them reverse their stances and grips and then swing the sword one hundred times left-handed. Did Sensei realize that Mitch and Max had not only discussed this deviation, in the interest of symmetry and proper exercise physiology, but had been practicing it on their own? Max glanced at Mitch. He winked back.

Sensei, usually one to economize his word usage, felt that some explanation was warranted. "We try to keep our aikido training modern. Our ancestors did not know that exercising only one side of the body can cause overuse injuries. Besides, every other activity in aikido is done with both left and right, so why not *bokken*? We seek balance."

Max wondered if he should tell Sensei how much he agrees with him . . . that he and Mitch drew the same conclusion a long time ago . . . that they have been privately engaged in iconoclastic behavior, both doing left and right sword cuts, for over a year . . . that they even execute left-handed golf swings from time to time. Hmmm. Discretion is good. Maybe later.

Mitch and Max decided to celebrate their newfound validation of bilateral sword-cutting by heading to a newly opened tavern, Brews R Us, on the outskirts of Rochester. For lightweight drinkers such as themselves, it's the quality, not the quantity, of consumption that counts. The new brew pub advertised more than two dozen beers on tap, so the guys were sure to find concoctions that suited their tastes. Max settled on Burgundian Brown while Mitch opted for Genesee Vanilla Porter.

"So, Sensei has seen the light," remarked Mitch, "not that I'm too surprised. He's a sharp fella, and our teacher—probably the main reason we train aikido."

"Yes, and I wonder how much of a conflict it was for him to introduce that left-handed *bokken* work tonight. He often invokes tradition, cites O-Sensei, and emphasizes the importance of practicing the fundamentals. And here he goes into what would be considered heresy by his Japanese brethren by introducing this anatomically correct change," Max added.

"Now that we've opened this door, Max, when do you think we should replace some of our right-handed golf clubs with some left-handed ones?"

"Gee, it could be done. There are plenty of switch-hitting baseball players."

"And think of all the times you have to hit from under a tree, or have to curve the ball in the direction opposite from your usual fade or draw."

"Maybe we're onto something, Mitch. Then again, I cannot think of a single professional golfer, tour or club, who swings from both sides of the ball."

"I once knew an amateur who did. I played in the Upstate New York Amateur at Birdies' Brook Country Club near Jamestown against a guy who carried, oh, maybe six left- and seven right-handed clubs."

"And his putter?" Max inquired.

"Twin-bladed, of course! I seem to recall that he putted lefty or righty, depending on the break."

"How well did he play? And what did *you* shoot, or shouldn't I ask?"

"I hit the ball great, especially from all those uphill, downhill, and sidehill lies that they have at Birdies' Brook. Our home course, Rolling Greens, gave me great preparation for that. But that guy made twice as many putts as I did. I could not adjust to the grain on those greens."

"So, again, how well did you score, Mitch?"

"The answer to that helps to explain why you are the pro, Max, and I am only an amateur."

Mitch was rescued from Max's inquisition by a ruckus in the far corner of the bar. A shriek by a young woman made the men turn around just in time to see what was at least a second punch being directed at a tall, slender young man by a much brawnier brute. Max and Mitch did not pause to discuss the situation; nor did they take the time to check for a reaction by tavern employees, especially when they saw two other guys within that section spring to their feet, appearing ready to join in the growing fray. They seemed to be siding with the aggressor. Mitch and Max slid off their barstools and glided quickly across the room as the attacker's third punch was partially deflected by the defender's arm; the force, however, knocked him down into the space between his table and a wall.

"Whoa, that's enough," Max said loudly and clearly. His swift, stern words worked. At least they sort of did. The big chap turned in his direction.

"Butt out, Bub," he bellowed with a drunken slur.

Max had *always* hated being referred to as "Bub." But rather than take exception to it, now perceiving the menacing faces of three strapping youths directing their attention his way, he remained calm enough to use his aikido training.

"That guy probably had it comin' to him," Max observed, affecting an inebriated slur himself, not to mock the big fellow but rather to connect with him, "but that's enough."

"Yeah," added Mitch, helpfully.

It wasn't a punch that came Max's way. Instead, the guy swiftly lunged his arms at his chest and shoulders, from down at his sides, in order to shove Max backwards. Max didn't have time to think of the attack's Japanese label, *ryokata-oshi*. He did, however, have the time and space merely to pivot aside, moving in toward his assailant, swinging his arms forward and upward in the same motion. As he dropped his right elbow upon the dude's left one, the man's balance was pitched forward. Max slid his right hand down his arm, hooked the guy's hand in his, then reversed his pivot and added the force of his left hand upon the top knuckles. The guy's knees buckled and down to the floor he went, onto his back, with a grunt. In close quarters among stools and chairs, Max had no room to finish the *kotegaeshi* maneuver by flipping him over, facedown, for a pin there. He merely added a little downward pressure to remind the bully that Max had painful control of his hand, wrist, and arm.

Mitch, meanwhile, had likewise managed a field application of aikido. One of the antagonist's companions had focused his gaze on Max and cocked a fist with Max's name on it. Mitch adeptly used both hands to swing the would-be assailant's other arm behind him; as Mitch ducked under his arm and came up again, the effective controlling hold, *sankyo*, swung the guy backward and well out of range of Max. The other buddy of the "bad guys," perceiving the ease with which his drinking partners had been subdued by Max and Mitch, showed no inclination to enter the fracas.

"Time to move to another table—*now*, please," Max said, without any fake drunkenness, to the initial victim and his friends. They nodded that they would comply without hesitation.

The concept of *zanshin* is an important one. It refers to "leftover *ki*," to the flow of energy that continues in the wake of an event, in this case an altercation. Mitch and Max simultaneously sought to keep the pressure on their captives in order to safeguard themselves, and to direct some benevolent attention their way in order to calm them and ensure their own safety. Aikido is purely a defensive art, one with the ethical intent of non-injurious protection of oneself and others. Max asked the big dude beneath him, "Are you okay?" Unable to read his look from the dark floor area, but feeling no struggle, he went on, "Let's let bygones be bygones. Besides," he added as another attempt at *aiki* communication, trying to harmonize with the thug's thinking in order to influence him, "our beers are getting warm and flat."

Mitch just patted his "partner" on the shoulder and extricated himself from the interaction with the comment, "It's cool, Bro." Max wished Mitch had called him "Bub." The three unruly patrons, now free to go, did so. Almost as swiftly as they had arrived on the scene, Mitch and Max returned to their bar stools. Were they calm and collected? Their breathing patterns indicated otherwise.

"Whew!" sighed Mitch. "I'm glad that our aikido training works so well, but I'd prefer never to use it in real situations."

"You've got that right," Max agreed. He breathed purposefully, striving to ease the adrenaline out of his bloodstream and back into the glands where it belongs.

The bartender thanked the guys for intervening in the fight and offered to give them brewed refills on the house. Max and Mitch concurred that glasses of water would serve them better than another round of beer.

Mitch sighed. "Now with that distraction aside, talk to me more about the murder theory. All that I could glean from the newspaper is that Pastor Puttnam's death remains under police investigation because of the deaths of the clergymen in Ithaca and south of Buffalo."

"Yes," Max confirmed, "and Detective Southworth disclosed to me that there was a similarly suspicious death along the Southern Tier, near Olean, a week or two ago."

"Holy cow! That's worrisome. Serial killings spreading?"

The altercation and its denouement had not gone unnoticed by the many patrons of Brews R Us that evening. Among the observers, seated at a booth ten yards from the fray, were Claude and Tony. The former, attired in a somber black suit with a dull gray tie to match, wearing a full beard and a Rochester Redwings baseball cap, seemed particularly spellbound by the incident.

"We could use guys like that in our group, Claude—tall, strong, and quick," Tony said as Max and Mitch returned to their barstools. "Our crusade needs skilled fighters. And they—"

Claude jumped in before Tony could conclude his thought, "Yeah, they made that look easy." He paused before adding, "We'll do fine with the crew we have."

Claude assembled his kindred spirits for a strategy meeting the following evening, Saturday, at an apartment in Lackawanna. Facing two new members of his organization, Holy Help (HH), he pondered his mistrust of strangers. Most people had been brainwashed by American culture, politics, religion, and the news media. He thought back in time to the many instances in which he felt he had been betrayed or belittled because of his beliefs. From his parents' scorn, to his teachers' criticism of his essays about the ills of society, to his pastor's rejection of his conception of God, Claude had been asked to lose face too many times. The radical ideas and religious fervor of his youth had persevered, but they were now tinged with anger and suspicion. Still, he wanted to expand his organization and influence, so he gratefully had a reason to expound upon the underlying principles of his cause. His voice changed from what he had used at Brews R Us, suitable for a clandestine discussion of dastardly deeds with Tony, to that of a divinely inspired preacher.

"My dear brethren, thank you all for coming," he greeted the dozen assembled men with a smug smile. "Our organization, as most of you know, is one of great importance and sanctity. By that I mean that our cause is righteous, serving our Lord and Master of our Universe in a way that is holier than that of the heathens and fake men of God who surround us." Claude looked down through his eyeglasses, past his pointy nose at his listeners in a direct and imposing manner. Able to talk circles around any of his verbally challenged disciples, he commanded their attention and respect. "We, as God-fearing Americans, know that we have certain inalienable rights—I think Abraham Lincoln said that—which are being threatened by our government, our churches, and even our so-called friends. But it is not merely our rights that we must defend, but also our duties to the Divine Creator."

One of the newcomers to the meeting, Billy, shifted uneasily in his folding chair. He had come along with his friend, Bruce, because he felt chronically disgruntled with his life. He doubted that any organization could be the answer to his woes, as Bruce had suggested, but he was willing to listen.

Claude continued, "We know that there is a Lord greater than that of Jehovah, Jesus, and Christianity. Our Lord is mightier than Allah and his servant, Mohammed. The Jewish God, the Asian Buddha, and the lords of the Hindus are merely manmade creations who pale in comparison to the Greater Lord whom we serve." What Claude would or could not describe were the erratic influences of his early childhood: regular church attendance with an assumption by his parents that he would heed its moral imperatives, too much freedom to do as he pleased since Mom and Dad were too self-absorbed to set limits and guide Claude, and unpredictable yet intense outbursts of anger and cruel punishment by both of his stressed-out parents when his minor misbehaviors tested their tolerance. Only tolerant treatment by most of his teachers, and sanctuary from his parents, kept him motivated to persist in school. Young Claude could make sense of his confusing world, and survive in it, only by twisting his perceptions of his unfair treatment. He went on, "The religions of the world, and the governments that serve them, are attacking us in countless ways: They tax the fruits of our labor, threaten to remove our right to bear arms, and pray to their gods in so many different ways that Our Lord is insulted and wrathful. They permit women to lead prayer. They pass laws to entrap us for no good reason. They control the press so that they can feed us lies and propaganda."

Billy was bright enough to sense that this speech was disjointed, but it had a compelling kind of logic that helped to explain some of the frustrations with which he lived. Besides, Claude sounded convincing, and those around him frequently nodded their assent to his words.

"We only live once, as far as we know. Why should we suffer the abuses that are directed at us? Why should we struggle every day, trying to make ends meet, being robbed by high taxes, feeling frustrations each and every day, and knowing that there must be some way to better ourselves and serve our Mighty Lord at the same time? What can we do?" He paused for dramatic effect. "We can be agents of change!" Claude pronounced the last six words slowly, pounding his right fist into his left hand with each syllable. His voice thundered with a force that belied his smallish physique. "Our number is small but growing. Our tools for change are few but powerful. Most importantly, our leader, the Almighty Lord of Jehovah, Allah, Vishnu, Buddha, and all of the false gods that surround us, wants us to win our sacred battle. He gives us help every step of the way. My inspirations, and yours, come from Him and are both *holy* and *right!* Our enemies *can* be eliminated! We can enlist more Holy Helpers to join us to right the wrongs, empower us, and make Heaven on Earth!"

The nodding of the men had gradually increased in vigor and was accompanied by mutterings of assent; now it gave way to raucous applause and a chorus of cheers. Billy felt elated and hopeful for the first time in years.

V

LESSONS

"GOLF IS A TARGET GAME," Max told the group of forty-four earnest faces gazing at him in Mitch's sport psychology class. That may not seem like a lot, but the room was full due to perfect attendance. Forty were taking Mitch's course for credit; four members of the golf team had managed to make it to Max's session at their coach's suggestion. Sport psychology had quickly proven to be one of the most popular courses at small, fitness-minded Confluence College. "Hence, your orientation, your focus of concentration, has to be objective, visible, and external. Or does it? Isn't golf supposed to be a 'mental game?' Isn't the 'inner game' of paramount importance? What do you folks think?" Max asked the class.

Max sought to remain calm and patient, scanning the room and awaiting a response, during the ensuing silence. The students, hoping that his questions were rhetorical, awaited Max's answers. He didn't cave; he merely rephrased his query. "Is golf primarily a game of external or internal focus?" He jotted the two key options on the classroom whiteboard.

As he further scanned the eyes, and downcast faces, before him, one student ventured a response by raising his hand. "External," stated a lad whom Max soon surmised to be one of the golf team drop-ins.

"Okay, it's mainly external," Max affirmed. "Tell us why you think that."

"Well, as you said, Mr. Azure, golf is a target game. You look at each shot, line it up, and try to visualize a good one."

"So, visualization is an important part of the process," Max clarified as he paced slowly back and forth in the front of the classroom.

"Take dead aim. I think it was Harvey Penick who said that," added another male student, presumably a teammate of the previous contributor. Most of the students were busily taking notes, partly to help them learn and partly to avoid having to speak up in class. "You see your target and visualize yourself hitting your golf ball to it."

Max nodded, pausing briefly in hopes that some discussion might start to snowball.

A female raised her hand. "Yes?" Max encouraged.

"But isn't visualization a mental process? In fact, what you perceive with your brain is more important than what you see with your eyes."

"Ah, yes indeed," Max agreed. "Harvey Penick, for those of you who don't know, was a famous golf instructor. His advice, to 'take dead aim,' meant to look carefully and methodically at your goal." Max's brain flashed to the idea of "take deadly aim" with local clergy in mind, but he quickly reoriented to his audience. "Striving for precise focus increases the probability not only of approaching the target with your golf shot, but of blocking out distractions along the way. Look exactly at where you want your golf shot to travel, not so much at the sand traps and water hazards nearby. You do this with your eyes, which, as you have stated," Max nodded at the coed, "are simply tools of the brain. One form in which we think is pictorial. We see where we are headed, and then trust our bodily actions to get us there."

Another hand went up. As Max gestured to her, a portly blonde wearing glasses and a genuinely interested expression asked, "So are you saying that golf is mainly external or internal?"

"Thanks for keeping my eye on the ball," Max smiled sincerely, "and I'm getting to that answer. First, let's try a little experiment." Oooh, that last word perked them up. Max had struck a popular chord among these budding psychologists. He pushed his tush off the table on which he had just been leaning in the front center of the room and then shoved the table toward a side wall. He piled atop the table the classroom lectern, his laptop computer, Mitch's briefcase, the one spare chair, and a student's backpack in order to build a sizeable heap. "Okay, I need a volunteer."

Nothing makes classroom eye contact disappear as rapidly as those words. Max thought consciously of his center, with his arms hanging calmly at his sides, as he looked around for someone to "bite" at the invitation. Seeing that Max was going to wait them out, the initially bold golf team member inched his hand upward. "All right!" exclaimed Max. "Come on down! What's your name?"

"Putter."

"Very funny," Max said to accompany the chuckles in the room.

"No, really. My actual name is David, but my nickname is Putter." His teammates affirmed this to the faces that turned their way.

"If you've earned that moniker due to your prowess on the greens, then good for you." Putter shrugged and grinned to indicate, modestly, that he had probably earned the nickname with his short game. "Okay, Putter, please stand over there near that wall." Max pointed to the wall opposite the tableful of clutter that he had constructed. "Look at the table. As soon as you are ready, I'd like you to close your eyes and walk briskly over to the table, getting as close to it as you can without touching it, and without peeking." Putter walked unhesitatingly across the front of the classroom, slowed suddenly a couple of feet from the table, and then took one more, short step forward. He stopped and opened his eyes to find himself only inches from the formidable obstacle. The students murmured their surprise and approval. Max glanced at Mitch and caught his wink.

"Way to go!" Max praised. "Who's next?"

A girl in the front row, tall, dark, and athletic-looking, stood up. "I'll give it a try." Although she started more quickly, and finished more hesitantly, the results were similar. Max had a few more students try the experiment, with one softly colliding with the protruding briefcase, one stopping a couple of feet short of the mark, and another walking right up to within one inch of the table. Then Max explained.

"The objective of this little exercise is to show that you can trust your brain. When your eyes spy an objective, even briefly, your perception sizes up what is needed to attain it. Even with your eyes closed, and hence no feedback concerning your progress, your body has programmed itself to move just the right amount. This experiment also shows us that the process of approaching a goal is both a physical and mental operation, both external and internal. The two processes are sequential and inseparable. They are complementary and synergistic." Max resisted any temptation to simplify his language and risk "talking down" to his audience. Still, he maintained eye contact with the students in order to gauge their level of understanding him. A few had returned to taking notes, but most were actively engaged in listening to him.

"In golf," he went on, "you not only want to look at your ultimate target, but also to visualize the path that your golf ball will take in order to arrive there. As you line up to hit or stroke the ball," Max said as he grabbed a putter he had brought and acted out his words, "you gather external information with your eyes then turn your attention inward in order to imagine or 'feel' your body executing the action. My eyes necessarily shift to the golf ball before me, effectively closing off my image of the target. But, just as you trusted yourselves to walk eight or ten steps with your eyes closed, I trust that my body will carry out the muscular actions necessary to achieve my objective." Max stroked an imaginary putt.

"So, golf can be as easy as walking several paces with your eyes closed, right?" Max asked, this time rhetorically, with a raised eyebrow. "There's something else, isn't there? In fact, it's a critical element of our discussion of sport psychology. Does my mind think solely in pictures? How else does it operate?"

Some blank, and some pensive, expressions reached his eyes. Max saw the "Aha!" experience brighten the countenance of a guy near the left wall. Max merely raised both eyebrows expectantly at him. "We think in words. Thinking is language-based."

"Exactly," Max confirmed. "In fact, my inner voice never shuts up. The stream of consciousness is a flow of words, soliloquys, dialogues, and songs—usually the most boring, repetitive tune I have heard recently, playing incessantly in the background of my awareness. Anyway, when it comes to golf, or any target game, or any activity for that matter, our 'inner game' consists not only of pictorial images but of words. Self-talk guides our actions. It's a key part of sport psychology and, what else, Professor Treasure?"

"Cognitive behavioral psychology," Mitch took his cue. "One popular means of psychotherapy consists of helping clients become aware of their inner speech and how their words shape their emotions and behaviors for better or worse. If we learn to say constructive things to ourselves, we increase the probability that we will feel good and behave in a positive and fulfilling manner."

"Left to its own devices," Max carried on, "my mind might race along from one topic to another or, at least, stray from focusing on a golf shot that I face. So, I try to follow a routine sequence of thoughts. I purposefully combine verbal with visual thinking in a goal-directed manner. I tell myself to look at the target, visualize the path of the ball, relax my body over the shot, imagine the sensation of executing the shot successfully, and let it happen. When I'm playing well, this chain of guiding thoughts becomes simplified to 'see it, feel it, do it.'"

Max enjoyed the rest of his hour with the class. He went on to apply the aforementioned ideas to sports other than golf, and then to academic success—for instance, visually recalling correct examination data from the professor's writing on the whiteboard or smartboard, or from the student's own notebook or computer. Even imagining good grades helps to activate the study skills needed to earn them. Max had time to touch upon the concepts of flow, being 'in the zone,' and some other key elements of sport psychology as they apply to performance enhancement. It was gratifying to have a few students linger after class, as Max restored the furniture to its original order, in order to ask him more questions.

"Teaching golf and aikido serves you well, Max," praised Mitch as they were departing the classroom. "You keep things lively and interactive."

"I feel charged up when I teach, Mitch, and I like large groups. The collective *ki* in the room energizes me to keep moving and to speak with expression. Our aikido training helps me to speak fluently, letting my words flow out naturally as I monitor how they are being received. I've seen you connect pretty darn well with your classes, too, Mitch."

"That's why I do it, Max," he confirmed. "Teaching is intense and satisfying."

Max added, "It's rewarding to be able to channel the natural anxiety of public speaking into useful energy." He paused before wistfully saying, "If only I could do that in a golf tournament, in front of a gallery."

"Take you own advice, partner," advised Mitch. "Just practice what you teach."

Priscilla dialed Mitch's home number, hoping to reach him instead of his voicemail. She had mixed feelings about his typical recorded greetings, finding some to be amusing and others to be too bizarre or tacky for her taste. *Uh oh*, she thought, as the ringing rolled on and ended. Mitch began singing in imitation of Bob Dylan's "Times They Are A-Changin'":

"Now listen good people and you will hear
An absentee message that sounds so darn queer
That you'll swear that while singin'
Mitch was gargling a beer,
And his sanity's rapidly fadin'.
Well, you'd better talk back soon
On your plasticine phone
For Mitch's brain is due for a trade-in."

Most of Mitch's friends had come to expect and appreciate his unique greetings. Strangers who called typically responded either with pregnant pauses followed by serious messages, or chuckles of mirth and noticeable regathering of their wits before speaking. Repeat calls, for replaying the message for self or friend, were not uncommon. Priscilla reacted with a tone of disdain.

"Holy heaven, Mitch, that is wholly ridiculous. We need to talk about your sense of humor and propriety, among other things. It's 6:15 now, and I should be around all evening. Thanks, Darling." She hung up and shook her head, wondering what, if anything, she was going to do with that man.

Mitch was a bit late arriving home from his office that evening because he was conducting an intake session for a new client. Mitch entered his office waiting area and found that the man had arrived punctually. Mitch's first impression was of a normal-looking guy, maybe in his late thirties, whose body language betrayed the signs of anxiety that naturally accompany a first-time visit to a psychologist's office. The man sat with his legs crossed, one hand absently stroking his ear, with one foot tapping on the floor.

"Hi, I'm Dr. Treasure. You must be Mr. Opus."

"Yes, I'm Edward. Most people call me Ed."

"Okay, Ed, welcome. Come into my office and make yourself comfortable." Mitch led the way to his door then stepped aside and waved Ed into the room ahead of him. He was about 5'9" tall, wore khaki sports slacks and a tan sweater vest, and had thinning brown hair. Reading Ed's eyes even as they turned to his face, Mitch anticipated his question and said, "Sit anywhere you'd like." Ed chose the cozy-looking armchair near the window instead of the sofa across the room. The hard-backed chairs at the table, at which Mitch conducted testing, played games with young clients, and carried out his paperwork, did not seem inviting to

Ed, or most other clients for that matter. Mitch picked up his clipboard and seated himself in the matching armchair in front of Ed.

After sharing a printed copy of his office policies and recording Ed's health insurance data, Mitch said, "I'm glad you're here. Let's just jump right in. Why are you here? What brings you to see me?"

"It's kind of a sensitive issue, a bit embarrassing. It's been on my mind for some time now, and, well, it's still a little hard to put into words. Is it true that our conversation is private?"

Mitch described his personal policy, and professional obligation, regarding confidentiality, including the legal and ethical exceptions to the rule: suicide, homicide, and abuse. He mentioned that he maintains case notes, for his own memory and brainstorming purposes, and gestured toward the case folder already resting nearby on the corner of the table. Nodding with understanding and acceptance, Ed proceeded.

"It's about sex, Dr. Treasure. I can't get enough of it. I can't get it off my mind for any length of time. I eye and analyze any reasonably attractive woman I see, quickly sizing her up as worthy of scrutiny or not. I look at her face, seek eye contact, and guess her age. I look her up and down, more or less discreetly. If she's appealing, within an old enough age range, I imagine how it would feel to be romantically involved with her."

Mitch, nodding in an understanding manner and smiling slightly during this soliloquy, reached tactfully for his pad and pen. He was not going to have to jump-start this conversation. Ed was bursting to talk about his "problem."

"I picture myself with her, stroking her smooth skin and contours. I get aroused with the fantasy of interacting intimately with her. I mean, this isn't just a weekly thing, or only once or twice a day, but ten or twenty times per day. And I'm happily married! I don't make love with my wife nearly as often as I'd like, Doc, but I love her and have stayed faithful to her. I just can't get my sex drive to calm down. I leer, not just look at women. Am I normal? Am I crazy? Did society do this to me? Are my hormones out of whack?"

"Whoa, slow down a minute, Ed. Having a sex drive, or libido, is normal. If yours is exaggerated, you may be experiencing ETS."

"ETS? What's that? Is it serious?"

"Elevated Testosterone Syndrome, Ed. Is it serious? Yes, it could be. Or at least it is driving you to distraction. Let me ask you for a few details."

Mitch inquired about how long Ed had been concerned about his "condition." He asked for demographic information—about job, education, health, and hobbies—and then refocused on the presenting problem by inquiring more about the marriage, the sexual fantasies, and any self-stimulation in which Ed might indulge. He noted the relaxation of Ed's posture and body language as he, the perceived expert, took over the pace and topic of their conversation. Ed appeared to be noticeably relieved at feeling understood. It took him a while, accompanied by evaporation of some of his anxiety, before he came back to question Mitch's tongue-in-cheek diagnosis.

"So, ETS is my problem? That's Elevated Testosterone Syndrome, you said?"

"Yes," Mitch clarified. "That's just a fancy, unofficial diagnosis of your sexual preoccupation and relatively high level of lust. We have a lot more to talk about, in due course, but let me just try to put your mind at ease for now. You're not 'crazy,' Ed. You're just crazy about heterosexuality and sensual experience."

As their initial session continued, and he learned more about Ed's all-too-common and natural fixation, Mitch realized that Ed wouldn't be there in his office if the obsession did not cross the line from being a normal and healthy libido to being a source of emotional discomfort and distress. It must be a source of conflict and guilt, as well, that could reduce Ed's levels of functioning and contentment in everyday life. Given Ed's talkativeness, and the growing range of issues that he gradually brought out, it was no wonder that the session ran well past the "clinical hour." That was okay with Mitch. He was used to it. Often too generous with his time, and usually someone whom clients found easy to talk to, Mitch had expected them to run over.

As 6:30 approached, however, Mitch summarized the session to Ed, outlined a treatment plan, and had him sign a statement of informed consent to carry out the plan together. He then assigned homework in the form of better marital communication and "date nights" with his wife. Then they scheduled their next appointment.

"Holy pizzicato! I sure hit that one on the sweet spot," gushed Sister Rotini in response to a solid seven-iron shot. Her voice was a blend of sweetness and forcefulness. "It feels strange to grip the club so lightly with my right hand, Mr. Azure, but it seems to help."

"It's a matter of relaxing your muscles as much as you can, Sister," Max explained, "and trusting that you will activate them just the right amount for the shot intended. By the way, feel free to call me Max."

Sister Rotini was a petite, healthy-looking young woman in her mid-twenties, Max would guess, with short black hair and attractive brown eyes.

"Okay, Max. It's just hard to let go of tension. I'm used to gripping the club tightly so I can control it and strike the ball hard."

"As you say it that way, it sounds logical, right? You thought correctly that you want the club to follow a prescribed path in order to hit your golf shots straight, consistently, and with authority. But, although it may seem paradoxical, you will achieve those goals better with smoothness and ease, with reasonably relaxed muscles and good timing, than you will with strength. Here's why."

Max took a six-iron out of her golf bag and assumed a stiff, rigid stance. He addressed the ball with nearly every muscle of his body taut. He showed her that he could hardly move in that uptight condition. "Activation of extra muscles, those not needed to execute a golf shot, interferes with my swinging the club. I need to free it up. When I let go of all tension," Max demonstrated with a deep sigh before re-addressing the ball, "and simply maintain my postural integrity, I can let my swing flow naturally. I trust that my hands won't get so loose as to let the club fly out of them. I just think about turning my shoulders back, letting the downswing begin when it's ready, and following through on balance."

Max waggled briefly then hit the six-iron shot straight toward the little green at the two-hundred-yard mark in the practice fairway. It landed just short and hopped up near the flag. Years of golf-specific weight training, together with the effects of wrist locks and sword cuts in aikido class, had made his wrists and forearms unnaturally strong. Golf is a game of tempo, but strength lends distance.

"Hmm, a pretty nice shot I had," Max commented. "Would you be interested in trading your women's clubs for my set, Sister?"

Sister Rotini smiled. Max thought that the religious life, with golf as a sideline, was serving her well.

"No, Mr. Azure—uh, Max—but I'd consider letting you play for me in the Interdenominational Open later this month."

"No can do, Sister. I could never pass for a nun, nor for a priest or monk, for that matter."

"So, just show me that swing once more please, and I'll do my best to copy it."

Max rephrased his key points, self-talking his way toward another good shot, then returned to the more traditional and comfortable position from which to deliver golf lessons. He stood in front of her, coached her into a good set-up, and then silenced himself in order to let her concentrate on the task at hand. A quick study, Sister Rotini hit the majority of the next dozen shots solidly.

"I was skeptical that a golf lesson would help me, Max, but I guess that you've made a believer of me." Their synchronous smiles and eye contact made them both feel good about life at that moment.

Mitch and Max ran through the woods around the golf course in the interest of cross-training, not in search of golf balls. But they had learned to wear shorts with pockets in case they happened upon some of the errant shots that inevitably left the fairways.

"Oooh, a Whizbang 90 Tour Professional Optimal Trajectory," Max announced aloud as he slowed to scoop it from a bed of leaves by a bush. "It's a keeper. Say, Mitch, could I interest you in caddying for me for the U.S. Open Qualifier at Birdies' Brook in early June?"

"The interest is there, Pal, but I'll have to look at my schedule. Are you sure you want me along? Might I be more of a distraction than a help?"

"I guess that depends on your sense of humor, and whether or not you could keep it in check that day. That exploding golf ball you teed up for me last year at the inter-club matches tickled my funny bone for a few seconds after the shock of hitting it, but losing the hole to my humorless opponent cut into my enjoyment soon thereafter."

"Yes, but you'd never trust me to tee it for you again, anyway, would you, Max?"

"You've got that right. But you have other tricks up your sleeve. Incidentally, I'm grateful that you let me experience the off-center golf ball on the putting green *before* the Central New York PGA Championship, rather than during the round. Once again, I'm not sure how forgiving my playing partners would have been. I mess up enough shots without needing meandering putts and penalty strokes to stoke my scores."

"Gee, it sounds like you'd rather *not* have me caddy for you," said Mitch, without a trace of guilt in his voice or expression.

"On balance, Buddy, you're good for me," Max praised with some reluctance. Praise too often triggers embarrassed humility, distraction away from good behavior, or, in Mitch's case, humorous retort. Max kept talking in order to head off the latter. "If you're feeling all right, let's take the long loop back to the clubhouse."

They trotted up the slope en route to the forest path that borders the thirteenth fairway. Mitch read Max's mind. "What's the latest on the mysterious death here? Have the police located any suspects yet?"

Max simply shook his head.

VI

RUMINATIONS & RATIONALIZATIONS

BILLY DID NOT NEED ANY PERSUASION to attend the next meeting of Holy Help. In fact, he had asked Bruce when it would be. The first meeting, which Claude and his parishioners had wrapped up with heart-warming prayer after deriding some of the evils of society, left Billy wanting more. The brotherhood's frustrations were his own. Billy still wanted to believe in God, but he felt so much rage that his faith was hanging by a thread. He was good at his job as an auto mechanic but felt treated like dirt. The service department of the car dealership took in seventy-nine dollars per hour, paid Billy a measly twelve dollars per hour, and claimed that the rest was needed to pay overhead costs. Customers rarely, if ever, praised his careful work. Neither did the service managers; instead, they criticized any little imperfection he made and pushed him to work faster. It was even worse than his teachers used to treat him in school—sometimes acknowledging his good efforts to compensate for his learning disability, but more often making fun of his silly mistakes and giving him poor grades. At least he had some friends now. Instead of being mocked by the regular students, particularly in eighth and ninth grades, who did not need special education, Billy enjoyed downing a few beers with guys like Bruce.

"Why do they—I mean, we—think that priests and reverends and guys like that are enemies?" Billy asked Bruce on the way to the meeting.

Bruce drove his beat-up old Chevy pickup truck that Billy helped keep on the road with his mechanical wizardry.

"That's obvious. They've lost their way. They no longer serve the Lord. They just serve all those people who crowd into their churches every Sunday. They ask for money from their audience and pocket it. They hurt our Lord by leading many people away from the path of righteousness." Bruce could not articulate, even if he knew, that Claude's messianic vision made him desire to cut down the competition for the spiritual hearts of Americans, leaving a void into which he and HH could sweep when the time was right.

"Oh," replied Billy in his usually succinct manner. "But what do golf courses have to do with it?"

"Gee, I don't rightly understand that part of it," admitted Bruce. "I kind of do, but maybe we better ask Claude today. He's a lot smarter about that stuff."

Claude swelled with pride as he looked out upon the group of fourteen men who chatted among themselves but, as soon as he began speaking, would hang on his every word. The larger that HH grew, even by one or two lost souls at a time, the more convinced he felt that his vision of the world was a just and righteous one. Not only did this group listen and cheer, but a select few of them did his bidding by attacking and eliminating the false prophets, the so-called holy men, the enemies of the Lord. Best of all, this was only the beginning. Over time, starting with this speech, Claude felt sure that his followers would increase a million-fold.

"Hello, my good men," he welcomed as he took his place behind the makeshift wooden podium, grasping its top edges with hands that trembled with a feeling of inner might. Claude wore a dark sport jacket over a gray open-collared shirt, striving to look authoritative while maintaining comfort. "I can see from the pained looks on your faces that many of you have had difficult times this past week. You have worked hard, been treated unfairly, and been given less credit than you deserve by your bosses, coworkers, and even your loved ones." Whether they had felt mistreated or not—even if they were unemployed and living on welfare—the men unanimously nodded and muttered their assent as they gazed with appreciation upon this wise and understanding man who stood before them. Applying the formal education he had received at the Massachusetts Polytechnic Institute (MPI), he spoke eloquently of their plight.

Glancing down periodically through his pince-nez glasses at his notes, Claude highlighted the dissatisfactions that he had observed in the lives of others, and felt in his own. In the process, he connected with his audience of malcontents and drove their collective emotional state into one of despair and anger. Then, he shifted his thrust to the topic of religion. He referred to a power greater than their own that could deliver them, and all their loved ones, from the miseries of life. He spelled out the primary source of the oppression they felt—the "political-religio complex"—and used his rambling logic to explain why clergymen are deserving of damnation rather than salvation. Among other things, he attacked the part-time nature of organized religion.

"Look around you at your brethren in this room. Are we not all miracles of life? Picture the splendors of nature—the mountains and valleys, forests and meadows, streams and deserts—that only the Lord above could have created for our pleasure. The Lord blessed us with bountiful good things, from food and shelter that enable us to live, to the beauties of nature for us to enjoy. He has always been with us, but look at what the countless members of organized religion believe. Most Christians worship only on Sundays, as though that is the only day that the Lord will hear our prayers, or that is the only day that the Lord deserves our thanks. The Jews limit themselves to Saturdays. All religions choose certain holidays to celebrate their views of God. Such religions are misguided! They insult the true Lord and King whom we hold in our hearts and minds seven days per week. The clergy of the world should pay for their hypocrisy, learn to be truly righteous, and teach our fellow Americans the true meaning of faith!"

Now with the audience in the palm of his hand, Claude felt bold enough to reveal the vehicle by which they could make inroads against the wicked establishment that governed their pitiable lives. He told how the Lord had conveyed to him the divine message—indeed, the command—to devote their lives to wiping out the false prophets among them, and then to spread the glory and prosperity of the Lord's Kingdom across the entire planet.

At this point, Claude declared, "I have plans. I will share some of them with you tonight. I need all of you to help me carry them out to the Lord's satisfaction. Yes, brethren, we will unite on a path toward contentment, not only for ourselves but for all those fellow human beings who are likewise superior enough to recognize our Lord as their Almighty. Our mission shall not surprise you, for we have begun to act upon it already, as most of you know. But before I proceed, I wish to hear any comments or questions you may have, my brothers."

Comments preceded questions. The vote of confidence for Claude was unanimous among them. Billy nudged Bruce to pose his question about golf courses, but Bruce shunned the attempt. Billy, feeling curious and emboldened because of the pleasant memory of having played golf with his father several times during childhood, felt no harm in asking. "Claude, sir, excuse me, but what do golf courses have to do with our mission?"

"Good question. I'll tell you, my son." Claude paused, took a long breath to gather himself for another persuasive speech, then proceeded. "Golf courses, and the game that is played on them, are a moral outrage. Golf is an elitist game, the folly of the wealthy. Rich men waste hours and hours of their time playing that silly game of hit-and-fetch while we laborers of the world toil away on their behalf. The game of golf produces nothing of value to the world. Country clubs build their courses on thousands of acres of land that could be far better used for hunting, fishing, farming, or housing. Golf course architects rape the landscape.

They destroy the habitats of wildlife, and of us humans, merely for the playing of their senseless sport. Then they cover the land with pesticides, herbicides, and a broad assortment of poisons. The golfers enjoy the scenery and lush grass, but the toxins wash away into our streams, wells, and drinking water." Claude, by this time, had worked himself into near fever pitch. "The greatest abomination, the biggest sin of all, is that our religious leaders, the so-called holy men who are supposed to lead us down paths of goodness and righteousness, also play the dreadful sport of golf. That is symbolic of all that is wrong with society! It is unforgivable! Our Mighty Lord, in His wisdom, has instructed us to do worthwhile things, to lead superior lives. We must show our fellow humans the error of their ways. We must protect ourselves from being enslaved and dominated by corporate and religious leaders who put us to work, pay us next to nothing, spoil our land, and make us pay their way to play golf!" He virtually spat that last word toward his audience. "Our sacred duty is to save ourselves and those who deserve salvation along with us! We must take action now!"

The baker's dozen in the audience stood as one, whooping it up with their fists in the air. The question-and-answer period was over. Claude had laid the groundwork for specifying their enemies, and he partially explained how to conquer them.

Max sat at his desk in the little office behind the pro shop during his lunch break on Sunday, thinking fondly of Melody. It was a challenge for them to get together often. Max wasn't always responsible for opening the pro shop at dawn, and closing it at dusk, but often enough to set himself up for many long days. The "work week" means nothing to a golf club professional. Weekends attract the most golfers and are, hence, the most opportune time for giving lessons, selling equipment, and making a living at the profession. But it had always amazed Max how many people are available to play golf during the week. Don't those people work? How can they find the hours necessary to play a round of golf at the expense of their jobs, household responsibilities, family interactions, and even other hobbies? His own "spare time" got absorbed by chores at home, aikido training three evenings per week, and exercise sessions; physical fitness is predicated upon cross-training, by a golf-friendly blend of aerobic, strength, and flexibility workouts. Throw in the hours of practice time and the occasional weekend golf tournaments in which he participated, and it was a wonder that Max could have any time at all for social life.

As for Melody, her schedule was almost as densely congested as his. A graduate of Syracuse University's S.I. Newhouse School of Public Communications, who developed a taste and flair for sportscasting at the school's FM radio station, she had landed a weighty job at WROC in Rochester. Hers was a terrifically diversified job there. Not only did she get to continue to cover sports, both local and regional, but she also had her hand in featured news stories. She was often dashing from one location to another to cover the latest breaking bit of sensationalism— from the occasional homicide to the discovery of some exotic species of shellfish in Lake Ontario. She did play-by-play announcing for Rochester's professional hockey team, broadcast sports news on both radio and television, and, as fate would have it, covered local golf tournaments once in a while. It was at the Monroe County Club Professional Championship that their paths had crossed for the first time nearly two years ago. Max knew that he had only himself to blame for ballooning from a tournament-leading sixty-seven the first day to a dreadful seventy-eight the next, but he liked to think that he was distracted by her interview of him after the first round.

It was Sunday. Things quieted down around the golf course by dinnertime. Janet would come on duty to manage the pro shop at 5:00. Max could play nine holes or . . . He telephoned Melody.

Mitch always had a "game plan." He never entered a counseling session without some sort of agenda. He hoped that each client brought issues, maybe even signs of improvement, to which he could respond in a here-and-now manner, but he dreaded "dead time" and feelings of going nowhere. Thus, he always perused his case notes in advance, reviewing not only what had transpired previously but also the mini-plan that he typically inserted into his notes to prepare for the future. A homework assignment to his client provided a good focal point, too.

Mitch now reviewed the file of JD Smith, the troubled and troublesome adolescent whom he had seen four times so far without the slightest sign of therapeutic improvement. JD's childhood had been marked by tantrums and oppositional behavior. When his overwrought parents began to receive reports from his preschool and kindergarten teachers that JD did not restrict his misbehavior to home, they were fully agreeable to having JD evaluated by the school psychologist. What followed were years of behavior plans and in-school counseling that enabled JD, a bright lad, to keep his head above water academically but failed to shape him socially and emotionally. Eventually classified as "emotionally disturbed" (ED), JD had received part-time assistance—mainly instruction in self-control and encouragement to do assignments—from special education teachers and school social workers. What ensued were more assessments, empty threats by his parents to send their only child to a foster home, and frustrations all around. A friend of a friend had steered the Smith family to Mitch.

His experience told Mitch that JD's parents were probably of one extreme or the other: too permissive or too punitive. Indeed, when he initially interviewed them, they confirmed the former hypothesis to be true. They confessed to letting JD shape his own early life. They gave their toddler too many choices, and set far too few limits, in the interest of letting his self-esteem grow unbridled. He grew unbridled, all right! Lacking the boundaries that teach him right from wrong and how to get along with others, JD was far under-socialized by the time he entered preschool. He was a terror in kindergarten, constantly wanting his own way and refusing to comply with classroom routines. He often ignored teacher requests, instead engaging in whatever struck his fancy—damaging property, violating personal space, spouting four-letter words, and routinely striving to be the center of attention. Not only did he misbehave, both impulsively and willfully, throughout his elementary school years, but he blamed others for most of his misdeeds.

Despite the apparently extreme and chronic history of JD's problems, Mitch was surprised that the increasingly intense educational and therapeutic treatments had not been more beneficial over time. Sure, the parents had helped to make a monster of their son despite their good intentions. But there had to be more to it than that; Mitch suspected that some trauma, negative peer influence, or health problem could be exacerbating JD's bad habits. Today, Mitch planned to question his parents further about his early development, then administer a self-report behavior rating scale to JD; the seventeen-year-old generally complied well with structured activities that fostered self-expression.

JD and his parents arrived five minutes late; the lad had "accidentally" broken a glass, thereby delaying their departure from home for the session.

"Howdy," greeted Mitch. "I'm glad that all of you could come today."

JD shuffled sulkily into the room and sank into the comfortable armchair. Mitch caught the expressions of disapproval flash across the faces of Mr. and Mrs. Smith just before they showed their social smiles and seated themselves on the sofa. As at past sessions, body language spoke volumes. JD looked neither at his parents nor at Mitch, but at the nearby wall; his crossed legs and arms showed that he was feeling unreceptive to anything to be said or done that day.

"JD, I'm glad that you're here, and I have something for us to do in a few minutes, but I'd like to speak alone with your parents for a while." JD started to rise by slapping his hands against the armrests of his chair. "Whoa, Bro! Not so fast," said Mitch with a smile and a clap on JD's shoulder. JD gave Mitch a fleeting moment of eye contact and almost grinned; Mitch may not have made any therapeutic inroads with the teen yet, but he had managed to establish some rapport during the three recent solo sessions with him. "Take along this box of colored tiles of various shapes. On the paper on this wooden tray, I'd like you to make something with the tiles—anything at all." It wasn't the standard way to administer the Lowenfeld Mosaic Test, but it would likely keep JD busily occupied for a while.

Following up on his hunches, data from the school, and the general information he had obtained from his intake session with the parents and times with JD, Mitch now asked specific questions of Mr. and Mrs. Smith. He discovered that JD acted colicky for months after birth. He resisted being held and avoided cuddling. Nothing seemed to make him happy for long. He had always eaten well enough but had slept fitfully throughout life thus far. Neither behavioral nor neurological assessments had revealed any compelling evidence of an attentional disorder, and his learning capacity had always seemed okay—when, that is, he was interested in what he was asked to learn. If his parents did not know better, they would swear that JD was *born* as a difficult child.

"I've already asked you some of this before. Tell me a bit about your parenting philosophy. How did you try to raise JD?"

"I guess that we tried to be liberated and liberating parents," replied Mr. Smith. "We wanted JD to feel good about himself—I remember reading something about empowerment—so we gave him lots of freedom to choose."

Mitch made no verbal comment, but simply looked to Mrs. Smith. "Gee, that's true. For his self-confidence and autonomy, we thought it best to let JD explore his environment freely. He wandered into some places he did not belong, both at home and in other places, and broke a lot of things. But we felt we were doing the right thing to try to keep him happy and let him be in control of himself."

"I'm sure that you did your best. Your intentions were great. But . . ." Mitch could not resist doing some direct instruction, even if it may have been too little too late. "Young children are, by nature, very self-centered. As an outgrowth of their early dependency on caretakers to provide for their needs, they tend to clamor for instant gratification. They love to seek attention and emotional reactions, positive or negative, from adults and peers, especially from the ones to whom they feel closest—you, his parents. I fear that your good-hearted attempts to placate JD by allowing his curiosity and impulses free rein may have contributed to his being under-socialized and feeling down on himself. Kids need, and like, limits. Parents communicate love by providing structure and boundaries, by caring enough to put up with the storm when you dare to say 'no' to a demanding toddler. Child-rearing is the process of teaching manners, self-control, and the social skills that we all require to build satisfying relationships with others."

"Holy heck, that explains a lot. We're sorry," lamented Mr. Smith.

"Don't sweat it," excused Mitch. "It's water over the dam. Nobody ever trains us how to be parents. Besides, you also did a lot to make JD the likeable young man that he can be."

"But, as your explanation would predict, he has always been a lot of self-centered trouble, too," added JD's mother.

At this point, Mitch learned some significant information accidentally.

"In fact," said Mr. Smith, "the only time that he was noticeably quiet and cooperative was when his mother was away when JD was an infant."

"You were away?" Mitch inquired of Mrs. Smith. "When and for how long?"

"Well, let's see, it was before JD's first birthday, so it couldn't have affected him very much. My father was ill, and so was my mother, so I had to go to Chicago to take care of them for a few months—until my mother had recovered enough to take over caring for Dad. He never recovered fully and passed away about a year later, before our poor little JD had a chance to get to know his grandfather."

"So, for three or four months, starting sometime before JD's first birthday, you were away?" clarified Mitch. Both parents nodded. "And you were his sole caregiver?" he asked the father.

"Yes, except that I had to work. But he didn't always give the babysitters a hard time. He'd often cry himself to sleep, especially at first, they told me. I did the best I could when I was with him."

Mitch now had a much stronger rationale to account for JD's so-cial-emotional difficulties and his resistance to positive change. Not only was he predisposed to having problems because of his early tempera-ment—personality tendencies that tend to persist over time—but had experienced a sense of maternal abandonment during a critical period of his early development. In some cases, children who endure broken bonding experiences with their significant caretakers for some time before the age of one suffer from "anaclitic depression," or "reactive attachment disorder," a potentially lifelong sense of loss and source of melancholy. Given his shaky start in life, and his parents' overly indulgent attempts to make him feel happy and empowered, it was now under-standable why JD's bad habits were so deep-seated. The self-report of behavior and personality that JD completed later that day, along with the preponderance of black and red tiles that he employed in his mosaic design, further indicated that JD was plagued by chronic anger, which, in turn, was rooted in depression. He may have acted mean and belligerent on the outside, but he was just a hurting, sad boy on the inside.

VII

CONTACTS & CONFLICTS

A FEW WEEKS HAD PASSED since the fateful final round of golf by Pastor Puttnam. In fact, the news contained no word of any more mysterious deaths at golf courses in the state. Max felt relieved at that. In fact, the incident had fairly left his mind as he teed it up with Mitch, Rabbi Greene, and Father Mulligan during the late afternoon of that Tuesday in mid-May.

"Okay, guys, we need to have a serious match today. Let's put some pressure on one another to see what we're made of," exhorted Max.

"But we already know that you're a creampuff, Max," retorted Mitch.

"Are you striving to prepare yourself for some event, Max?" asked the rabbi. "Are you trying to get tournament tough?"

"Exactly. I know in my heart, head, and hands that I have the game to make it into the U.S. Open this year. I feel determined to qualify this time."

Their conversation paused long enough for Father Mulligan to sky his first drive to a point just past the women's tee. As he teed up another ball, Mitch asked, "I know you told me before, but I forgot—where's the qualifier being held this year?"

"At the country club near Jamestown at which you once played—Birdies' Brook."

"Nice name, especially if you can score a lot of those," reacted Mitch. "When I was there, I learned that the name was based as much on the nearby museum of a famous bird fancier, artist, and naturalist, Roger Tory Peterson, as on the goal of the golfers there. Are birdies easily made there? Not really. As I told you before, the course is wholly hilly, which makes for some interesting lies, and the greens are tough to read." Mitch hit a solid drive down the right center of the fairway. "Do you still want me to caddy for you?"

"Hit 'em like that, and I'll want you to play in my place. Yes, Mitch, if you're available."

Their round together did *not* manage to resemble the tension-packed atmosphere of a tournament. The clergymen may have enjoyed the game of golf as a worthwhile challenge and diversion, but they could not take competition too seriously. Neither could Mitch, based upon the cooperative manner of their aikido training and his psychological belief that harmonious interactions are healthier than competitive ones. So, they played a laid-back game of "high-low," the rabbi and Max against Mitch and Father Mulligan. Only a round of soft drinks rested on the outcome. Still, despite the low stakes, their keeping score of the contest made them all focus a bit more sharply on their shots and putts.

"Drat, I should have made that one," groaned Rabbi Greene after missing a six-foot putt on the seventh hole.

"Who says?" Max queried.

"I beg your pardon."

"Who says that you should have made that putt?" Max clarified. He was not trying to challenge or annoy his playing partner. He simply felt like exploring a topic that had troubled him for all of his years of golf. "I just mean that all golfers, you and me included, feel that we 'should' have made a putt, 'should' have hit a straight drive, 'should' not have hit a shot into the water hazard, and so on. We often sum up a day's round with a statement like, 'I shot eighty-two, but I should have shot seventy-seven. If I had only avoided those two three-putts, made that two-footer for par, and not hit out of bounds, I would have shot seventy-seven.'"

"Ah, those good old 'should'ves,' 'would'ves,' could'ves,' and 'ifs,'" chimed in Mitch. Rabbi Greene waited patiently, shaking his head bemusedly, for a chance to respond. "Yes, indeed, my scores are always higher than they 'should have' been."

The rabbi opened his mouth to speak, but Father Mulligan jumped in first. "Maybe I ought not to say this, but we do make too many excuses for ourselves, don't we? Not just on the golf course but in all walks of life, people tend to feel that they could be doing better, rarely measure up to their own expectations, and would do better 'if' someone or something fateful had not interfered. Of course, in the confessional, I cannot tell you how many times my parishioners have begun their statements with 'I know that I shouldn't have . . .' or 'I should have known better, but . . .'"

Rabbi Greene raised his hand for permission to speak as they walked to the eighth tee, but the guys ignored him some more.

"The 'shoulds,' 'oughts,' and 'coulds' are endemic to our culture," observed Mitch. "The well-respected psychological theorist and therapist, Albert Ellis, strove to help people to stop torturing themselves with what they 'should' be or do; he preached reality and rational thinking along with acceptance of our human fallibility."

"On the other hand," Max said as Rabbi Greene cleared his throat, loudly, as if to speak, "you have previously told me, Mitch, that research has shown that optimism, feeling that things 'should' go well for us, is correlated with good mental health."

"Yes, that's true," Mitch responded. "The happiest, healthiest people maintain an illusion of well-being, deluding themselves with self-serving biases and rationalizing away most of their shortcomings."

"I should have made that putt!" Rabbi Greene interrupted the discussion. Everybody laughed.

"Well, yes, you should have," Max agreed. "It was a straight, uphill putt. Your miss cost us a point."

Rabbi Greene hung his head in mock shame. All eyes were on him. He looked up, glanced from face to face, and then seized his opportunity to speak. "And who says that I should have made that putt—besides you,

Max, and me? Certainly not God. He has better things to do than to watch over my putts. In fact, I often wonder whether God thinks that I have better things to do than to play golf."

"I wonder that myself," added Father Mulligan.

"Me too," agreed Mitch.

"Count me in," Max said. The three gentlemen looked at Max with surprise.

"But you, Max," the rabbi articulated all of their thoughts, "you're a golfer. This is your chosen profession."

"Yes, but when you analyze the game of golf, you have to wonder whether it's not merely a tremendous waste of time, effort, money, human energy, spinal health, and natural resources. We spend hours per round, and countless days of our all-too-brief lives, torqueing our backs to swing at a ball, knocking it toward a target, and totaling how many times we've done it. Is it truly meaningful? Does it better the lives of others, or even our own? As you just said, Rabbi: Couldn't I, and shouldn't we, find better things to do with our lives?"

"For our own mental health, and for the sake of finishing this round, let's delude ourselves a bit," replied the psychologist in their midst. "If I may, please allow me to quote Arnold Palmer: 'Golf is deceptively simple and endlessly complicated. It satisfies the soul and frustrates the intellect. It is at the same time rewarding and maddening—it is without a doubt the greatest game mankind has ever invented.'"

"Hallelujah," responded Father Mulligan.

"Amen," agreed Rabbi Greene.

"Not to mention that games serve a valuable purpose," Max said, in apparent contradiction to his own quandary. "The quality of life depends upon a delicate balance of work and play. We need recreation and leisure for the purpose of stress management. In pursuit of a sense of competence, no better game exists than golf—a blend of physical and mental challenges that change from course to course, hole to hole, and day to day."

"Shall we play?" invited Mitch. He hit one straight and long. "I hit that one on the sweet spot; I felt the tingle from the clubhead all the way to the pleasure center of my brain. *That* is why we play golf." Onward they went, each striving for such sweet shots.

After twelve holes, Rabbi Greene and Max were two points behind their opponents. The afternoon breeze had come up. Despite the forest lining the thirteenth hole, the wind penetrated enough to coax Max's drive into the left rough. Mitch followed suit, while the rabbi sprayed his tee shot to the right. Only Father Mulligan, by hitting his natural fade, managed to steer the ball down the middle of the fairway. In preparation for his second shot, the priest bent down to pluck some grass with which to get a rough reading of the wind's direction and velocity. "Whizz! Knock!" They all heard it. A projectile must have streaked through the air and popped into a tree trunk in the woods. Indeed, a golf ball rebounded back into the rough and rolled to a halt. Max looked toward Father Mulligan and saw him face-down on the grass. The priest turned his head toward Max and Mitch and, with eyes wide, said, "What in the name of the Holy Ghost was that?"

Max scanned the forest across the fairway and, somewhat past Rabbi Greene, detected movement in the underbrush. With his seven-iron in hand, he took off running in that direction, exhorting Mitch with a quick, "Come along, partner!"

Mitch had other plans. He must also have sized up the situation, and seen the nearby movement, but he was running back toward the tee. *Thanks a lot, pal*, thought Max.

As Max reached the edge of the woods, he caught a glimpse of what appeared to be two men heading away, the lead guy loaded down with something in his arms. Max thought of shouting to them to stop, in the hopes that they might at least turn toward him so that he could see their faces. But he stayed silent, hoping not to panic them into fleeing faster. In spite of his athletic training and stamina, Max already felt mildly winded from the rapid onset of the chase. Slowly he gained on the guys, but going through the underbrush was tough. As he neared one of the cross-country skiing and running trails that parallel the golf course, Max detected none other than Mitch off to his right, bumping along in a golf cart that was ill-equipped for off-course travel. Jostled by tree roots, holding onto the steering wheel with both hands, his head bounced along with a look of, *Why am I crazy enough to be doing this?* on his face. Max grinned despite the tense circumstances.

Max crossed the trail and continued toward his objectives. Mitch, contrary to expectation, did not stop the cart and join in the footrace. Max heard the cart behind him, crossing to his left. Of course, that path eventually met the nearest road, so maybe . . .

One of the men ahead turned to glance at Max. They surely knew that he was giving chase, and Mitch's cart added telltale sound. Drat! Max saw a car up ahead and realized that the guys would reach it before he could close the gap between them. The one in front, carrying the lengthy object, arrived there first, opened the trunk, and dropped his load inside before slamming it and heading toward the driver's door. The second man had stopped and turned around, fixing a menacing gaze upon Max, who had slowed to pant heavily due to his exertion. The guy was a big dude, wearing a green sweat suit, with fists clenched. As he heard the car's engine start, Max also heard the familiar sound of the little engine of a golf cart putt-putting toward the scene from his left. "Mitch, really? You expect to run them down in a golf cart?" Max muttered to himself.

Just as the oversized guy turned to open the passenger door of the car, it sped off down the road. He shouted, "Hey!" at the vehicle without effect. Apparently, the driver did not take partnership very seriously. As he turned to face Max again, the man caught sight of Mitch, bringing his golf cart to a halt and leaping from its seat. Words cannot describe the look on that man's face! Abandoned by his partner, and now cornered by two pursuers—one breathing heavily, with a golf club in his hand, and the other, taller than the first, advancing calmly with a look of satisfaction on his face—the guy stood with eyes wide, lips curled, labored breath, and an expression of bewilderment. The look soon changed, however. He now gritted his teeth, re-clenched his fists, and took on the demeanor of a beast that has been cornered for a life-and-death fight.

"Be cool, man," said Mitch. "Stay calm. Let's talk."

Having slowed to a walk as soon as the car had exited the scene, Max now stopped a couple of yards away from the man. His bodily tension showed no sign of easing up. He reached down to the shoulder of the road beneath his feet, grabbed a fistful of gravel, and pitched it at Max before lunging toward him. Max dove to his right, doing a nifty shoulder roll with his seven-iron still in hand, and came up facing the guy with the weapon poised above his head and ready to strike. The guy was startled. But rather than drop his fists and surrender, he whirled around and swung in Mitch's direction. Mitch had indeed approached within striking distance, but merely ducked to avoid the roundhouse punch. Aikido isn't always hands-on; students also practice *tsudori*, a quick maneuver to get off or below a line of force.

The opening was now Max's. He dropped the golf club and hooked both hands over the shoulders of the man, one on either side of the back of his neck. Max swiftly slid them up, backward, and down along the back of the guy's shirt. The big thug quickly lost his balance, sat down roughly on his bottom on the shoulder of the road, and bumped the back of his head on the grass-covered ground. As he sat up, visibly dazed, he saw Mitch and Max standing before him with their hands open at their sides and looking ready to defend themselves.

"Chill out," Max advised. "It's over."

This time, breathing more heavily than ever and feeling both betrayed and bamboozled, he relaxed a bit. "Shoot," he muttered.

Max and Mitch offered him the chance to walk on his own, between them, back toward the golf clubhouse, or to have them apply an uncomfortable wrist lock to move him along. He chose the former.

As they reentered the thirteenth fairway, they were approached by Rabbi Greene, members of the group who had been playing behind them (from whom Mitch had borrowed the golf cart), and Father Mulligan. The priest had a minor abrasion visible on his right temple. The golf ball missile had merely grazed him, thanks to his timely duck.

"Did this man shoot at me?" asked the Catholic clergyman without any hint of malice in his voice.

"Apparently, yes, if not his partner—the one that got away," Max replied.

"I'll pray for you, my son," responded the holy man reflexively.

"Yeah, right, thanks for nuttin'," responded the culprit sarcastically.

Mitch directed one of the golfers to the cart he had left on the road, and another rode the group's other cart to the clubhouse to call for the police, while the walkers proceeded across the course with their clubs and their captive.

Detective Southworth telephoned Max the following morning. "That guy you captured wouldn't say much about how you nabbed him—he wouldn't say much about anything for that matter—and I myself wonder how you guys did it. There's not a scratch on him. But he doesn't look like the type of guy who would give up without a fight. Some facial scars suggest that he has been quite the ruffian over the years. How'd you and your friend do it?"

"Mitch and I train aikido, a nonviolent art of self-defense. I guess that some of it works pretty well. We just persuaded him to come along once his accomplice had abandoned him."

"Yes, and your description of that guy—or lack of one, I should say—has gotten us nowhere. We found the car but haven't been able to trace it to anyone yet."

"That's too bad," Max said. "I sure hope that you can get to the bottom of this soon. Hasn't the big guy told you anything useful?"

"No, he seems to be under some code of silence. He's a stubborn cuss. All he would tell us, probably 'cause he got tired of our calling him just about everything in the book, is that his name is Frank. But we'll find out something. It'll just take time to learn about him by investigating his background and connecting with his social contacts. In the meantime, thanks for helping me do my job. Let me know if you recall any more about the other guy and what he was carrying."

"Sure thing." Max bid him adieu and hung up the phone feeling more of a nagging sense of frustration than of gratification for having caught one uncooperative perpetrator.

"Oh, boy," muttered Mitch in his empty office. "It's time for another session with Leonard Tourette. That guy sure makes me nervous. So much so, in fact, that here I am talking to myself." He smiled, sighed, and reviewed his game plan for Len.

There were three knocks on the door that connected his office with the waiting area. Mitch paused, knowing that four more, then another five, would soon follow. He wanted to help Len to abandon such rituals, but the price of this little one in terms of Leonard's anxiety just seemed too costly to pay at this time. At least he had managed to pare down the routine from its original two-minute sequence of knocking.

"Hi, Len." The client, a wiry thirty-four-year-old wearing a neat gray suit and black shoes beneath his deep brown, wavy hair, merely nodded his return greeting and proceeded to pace the floor the usual six times before sitting opposite Mitch.

Mitch thought back bemusedly once again to the public television documentary, *Twitch and Shout*, that profiled cases like Leonard's. Unfortunately, Len's darting eyes caught sight of Mitch's brief smile and, ever-sensitive to how people react to him, he asked, "What are you laughing at, Dr. T?"

"Oh, Len, I just permitted myself a little smile of enjoyment. You are one of my liveliest clients, and I'm glad that you're here." Aikido training gave Mitch practice reacting quickly to various physical situations; fluid thinking also applied to psychological counseling and empathy. It wasn't exactly a lie, either. Sure, Len made Mitch feel nervous, but he also felt energized by the challenge of staying calm and finding the means to make therapeutic inroads.

"Tell me how your week went."

"Oh boy, oh boy, do you really want to know?" Before Mitch could even nod, Len continued in his fast-talking Brooklyn accent. "Work was good, just fine. I did some good stuff. The boss liked my ideas for a particularly sticky advertising campaign." Mitch trusted this to be true. With Len's consent, Mitch had touched base with his employer and found that, given a little extra space and leniency, Len was a valued team member of a local marketing agency. "But when I asked the foxy little secretary down the hall for a date, she could only giggle at me. I don't think that she meant to hurt my feelings. Maybe I'm just such a funny guy that she couldn't control herself. That's cool. It's nice to be amusing. But I never got an answer from her. She's got a nice laugh. It's good to hear. But when is she gonna answer me? That's what I want to know." Len's hairy head bobbed and weaved, and his hands gestured animatedly, as he spoke.

Mitch nodded agreeably. Sometimes he felt as though his head were on a spring, like one of those bobblehead dolls that bounces up and down when you tap it. With Len, who could barely allow Mitch or anyone else a chance to get in a word edgewise, nodding was all he could do until Len's soliloquy had played itself out.

"And I think that she likes me. She even said that I'm cute." Len rose from the chair in order to pace his skinny body back and forth across the office six more times. "Drat! Shoot! Fudge! Holy fruitcake! All I want is a date. I asked her to go out for coffee after work. Is that too much to ask?"

Mitch knew that he had a previous psychologist to thank for re-shaping Len's exclamatory vocabulary from one of vulgarisms to more socially acceptable language. "Gee, Len, it sounds like you have the start of something with that gal, but it's just moving too slowly and trying your patience."

"Yeah, yeah, maybe you're right. She does seem to enjoy my little visits with her. I've only asked her out three—no, four—times. She almost said yes, I think, but . . . maybe I'll talk to her again tomorrow."

Mitch liked his clients to speak openly and guide the session's agenda, and to take control of their own lives, but he often felt things spin out of control with Len. It was hard to keep up with the little dervish! *Do no harm*, Mitch thought to himself. Eventually, Len would always give him a few opportunities to jump in with some constructive feedback.

The session raced along in its usual manner, with high-strung Len giving more than taking. That was better than some of his silent, suffering, parasitic clients, thought Mitch. By the time they were done, Leonard had experienced some insight into how breath control might reduce some of his compulsions. He already knew that he could deflect his self-doubts with some positive self-talk. He had chosen a strategy for approaching the young lady on whom he had his eye. And Mitch felt exhausted as if he had just seen four clients back-to-back.

Len paced six laps, approached the door in order to knock his way out, but glanced back at Mitch. He redirected his hand to the doorknob to let himself out. "Yes!" exclaimed Mitch in a whisper, clenching his fist and pulling it in toward his bowed head, gesturing as though he had just made a big putt in a golf match. Progress, to any degree, is sweet.

JD was due in ten minutes. But he did not show. Twenty minutes into their allotted time, Mitch telephoned his home. Mrs. Smith reported that JD had called her after school to say that he would get to Dr. Treasure's office on his own—not to worry. Now, of course, she was worried. It was not until Mitch checked his office voicemail messages three hours later that he was relieved to hear from JD's father that the lad had returned home safe and sound. He had an excuse that, on the surface, was believable. Mitch felt disappointed about JD's no-show because their rapport had continued to grow stronger; ditching a session was not a good sign. He looked forward to next week when a joint session with JD and his parents was scheduled.

JD naturally gravitated toward Mike. In school, as elsewhere, misfits often attract. Unlike JD, who was ostracized by peers because of his sarcastic manner and disruptive antics, Mike was socially isolated due to thick glasses and learning problems. Too uncoordinated and visually limited to participate in sports, even in physical education class, and unable to earn passing grades except in special education courses, Mike had become a loner. Even JD had thought he was a nerd until he noticed some of Mike's artwork a few weeks earlier. Hunched over his desk, doodling instead of writing his assignment, Mike could draw caricatures of teachers that expressed both humor and frustration simultaneously. In the same special education program that year, though for different reasons (one couldn't while the other wouldn't do his work), Mike and JD had begun to relate to one another as friends. When Mike asked JD to blow off his appointment with his shrink in order to attend a gathering of some cool dudes, JD hesitated only briefly before concocting the white lie that he would tell his parents to pave the way. Mike said it had something to do with HH, the initials that he sometimes included in his stylized doodles. They would be going along with Mike's older brother, Luke, and his friend, a young auto mechanic named Billy. JD was perfectly willing to keep the event a secret, given Mike's assurance that he would feel much better about life after the meeting.

A third-degree black belt named Theodore Seidokai usually taught the first hour of aikido class on Wednesday evenings. Kikai Sensei was typically present, as well, but stayed in his small office doing paperwork. He trusted his assistant instructors and didn't believe in meddling in their lessons; he wasn't above a little eavesdropping for the purpose of some constructive criticism later, but he let the instruction and interaction flow.

Theodore, a short but powerful man of Japanese-American descent, was a graduate student at the University of Rochester. A cellist, he probably strove for perfect performance if his aikido style was any reflection of him. Theodore helped his students to examine some of the fine nuances of their aikido arts. They analyzed small movements, stances, and hand positions, determining exactly how to blend with a partner in order best to neutralize his or her attack. Max and Mitch always enjoyed his classes. His soft-spoken elegance was a pleasure to behold and worthy of emulation. They got plenty of rough-and-tumble training from Kikai Sensei and some of the other assistant instructors.

Theodore called for his *uke* with whom to demonstrate the next facet of his lesson plan: "Max, please."

Max said, "Hai," bowed from his seated position in line with his fellow students, then sprang forward to engage in the prescribed attack.

"*Katadori*," he requested, so Max grabbed one of his lapels and proffered a fist with which to threaten his face.

"That's it. Hit 'im, man!" came the voice from the front door of the dojo. Their school had apparently captured the attention of three male passersby who were looking for some action.

Max relaxed his grip on Theodore as the instructor replied to the heckler, "Good evening, gentlemen. You are welcome to enter and watch quietly."

Ah, ever the genteel Theodore, Max thought.

"Are we welcome to take over for that guy and punch you?" inquired a second, and tallest, member of the belligerent trio.

"As you have heard, you are welcome to observe quietly." This time it was the deeper, but equally polite, voice of Kikai Sensei that responded. "If you want trouble, then you are not welcome to stay," he added in a calm voice, but in a tone with a bite to it.

The three guys lingered in the doorway. They chuckled to each other, the first one saying, "Check out the little Japanese dude."

Sensei stopped his advance near Max and Theodore, stood stock still with his arms relaxed at his sides, and advised, "Either stay quietly, or leave peacefully."

Now the intruders seemed to notice the eight or nine students who sat in a line watching the lesson. The trio started to shift about nervously, as though in a synchronous dance with one another. They were not used to having their attempts at intimidation met with unmoving confidence. They glanced at one another's faces before the tall guy said, "Well, you guys don't look so tough, but we gotta go. Maybe later." They backpedaled out the door and headed down the street talking loudly, probably boasting about how they could have whipped those aikido folks.

"Extra lesson for tonight—winning without fighting," pronounced Sensei before wheeling back toward his office.

Max grabbed Theodore's shoulder, aimed his free fist at him, and then felt himself getting smoothly yet effectively led into a pin on the mat.

VIII

STROKES

THE MENU AT THE TURKISH BATH, a restaurant in Amherst, New York, specializing in exotic soups, appealed to Claude's taste that evening. Besides, the off-the-beaten-path place offered low-cost meals served in an uncrowded atmosphere that was conducive to private conversations. In their corner booth, Claude sipped on turkey noodle curry soup while Tony slurped up some ginger wonton consommé.

"What now, Claude? How am I going to continue without Frank?" asked Tony, perhaps eating faster and more sloppily than usual because of the upset of having lost his friend and partner. Maybe he also suffered from a trace of guilt for having hastily abandoned that partner at the scene of his capture. "And what if he tells the police about us?"

"Shhh," cautioned Claude, taking an extra look around to make sure that no one was within earshot. "Your mishap was most unfortunate, yes. But there is no need for panic."

"Maybe not for you. I almost got caught myself. I can't believe those two guys actually chased us." Tony stuffed a wad of bread into his mouth.

"It was just a bad break. We'll plan more carefully next time. And we'll stay away from that Rolling Greens golf course for a while," reassured Claude. "For now, I trust Frank. It's been two days since he was captured and there's no word in the media, or action by the police, to suggest that he broke our oath of silence."

"Yeah, but what if they find a way to trace Frank to us? And what if they trace the car I ditched?"

"All the vehicles we use are clean. I've taken care of that. It is possible, I suppose, that Frank has friends or relatives that the police could find who might know something about his joining HH. But, as you well know, most of our flock consists of solitary 'lost souls' such as yourself."

"I've noticed a bunch of new faces at the meetings lately. Is every one of 'em clearly on our side?"

"Ours is a glorious mission, Tony, ordained by the Lord above. The souls we save along the way are surely meant to be with us. I'm very pleased with the growth of our organization. I feel that every one of them, little by little, can eventually become full-functioning members of the group."

"You mean that you plan to have more of us out gunning down the holy folks?"

"Yes, eventually. When they have taken the oath of allegiance to the Almighty and our religious brotherhood, and I see that they are trustworthy, we will put together more teams of 'societal cleansers.'"

"And where do I fit in?" asked Tony as he chewed a bit of wonton behind a cocky grin.

"I like two men per team—no solo acts. I have a new partner in mind for you, or you may have ideas of your own. Maybe Frank will be released. Let's discuss it after the meeting this weekend."

Max had not seen his kid brother in nearly a year. Life just tended to get too busy, even for a trip as short as that to Western Massachusetts. He wondered if their parents felt even more guilt; since their full-time move to Florida four years earlier, in the wake of numerous family vacations there over the years, they had probably seen Zeke only once or twice. Max wondered if, within his social cocoon, Zeke felt as hurt as "normal" people would in the same boat. Maybe he would ask him. Max had an opportunity to drive to Pittsfield for an overnight stay before heading back into the Syracuse area for the next tournament in his golfing schedule.

The Massachusetts Colony for Youth (MCY) served individuals with a wide range of mental health issues. That was a good thing, too, since Max felt that his brother's label of Autism Spectrum Disorder (ASD) was only a "best fit" diagnosis. In many ways, Zeke functioned better cognitively and creatively than peers under the same diagnostic umbrella. But some of his quirky shortcomings caused him problems above and beyond what might be expected for a twenty-year-old with a history of this pervasive congenital syndrome. MCY met his needs for intellectual stimulation while trying to teach him the social and self-help skills needed to live successfully and happily within mainstream American culture. In his case, happiness never seemed to be a concern for Zeke. Indeed, when Max arrived to see him, there was Zeke gleefully playing a game by himself on the extensive lawn in front of the main building.

Max parked his car in the visitors' lot and, with a nod from the nearby caretaker, walked up to Zeke.

"Hi, Bro."

"Hi. Don't you love the way a frisbee soars into the sky then zips right back down to you if you throw it right?" It wasn't that Zeke did not recognize his brother. Rather, it was as though the two of them had never been parted.

Max joined right in. "It's also neat the way you can make it hover." He advanced to his brother and gave him a hug. Zeke responded, though stiffly. He broke off the embrace after only a second. Max asked, "How about a game of catch?"

His visit with Zeke that day was fun. There was no way that Max could wedge an awkward question about his feeling hurt, abandoned, or shunned by his family into the brotherly interactions. Why bring him down? When Max broached the subject with Zeke's caseworker, however, she agreed with Max's intuition that Zeke was experiencing a sense of loss of family. Yet he was coping all right. She reported that Zeke was responding as well as could be expected to the functional living skills training. The plans for his moving into a semi-independent living situation, and performing gainful employment as a minor civil servant, were set for the year after he turned twenty-one.

Early the next morning, after giving him a nifty frisbee that he had bought in one of the local college sporting goods shops, Max and his brother shared a warm farewell—a lengthy but speechless handshake.

"Do you like it here, Zeke?"

"I like it here."

"You're glad to be here?"

"I'm glad to be here."

Though not fully echolalic, Zeke's responses tended in that direction. Max saw that his brother looked healthy and fit. The day before, he had witnessed Zeke in the process of reading a John Steinbeck novel and working to publish some of his own poetry in the MCY print shop. Max felt convinced that his brother's needs were being met. With his heart in bittersweet mode, Max took his leave from his sibling to head for the highway and his next golfing adventure.

Max had been looking forward to The Club Special for weeks. Not only was it the unofficial championship of the teaching pros of New York State, with some strong competitors in the field, but it was worth getting excited about the prize money. Besides, it was a good tune-up for the U.S. Open Qualifier in two weeks.

It took him only one-and-a-half hours to reach the course outside Syracuse, Dimples and Divots, that was hosting the competition. Since he had never played there before, Max decided to devote the majority of his warm-up time to the putting green. He wanted to get the feel for the pace, and try to detect any grain or other tendency for putts to break systematically in any one direction. He also wanted to gauge the specific knowledge and support of his caddy, a local high school student who apparently played at that course when he wasn't caddying for special events there.

On the first tee, Max thought about the many high school golf matches that he had begun with either a top, skull, or scuff. Having reassured himself that it was alright to experience such a memory without having it affect his present tee shot—after all, he was now an accomplished golf professional—Max proceeded to drive the ball 130 yards along the ground. Rather than get down on himself, however, he stroked a long iron to within 100 yards of the green, hit a good wedge shot, and sank a twenty-foot putt to save par.

"Nice putt," muttered his taciturn caddy, Chip. He may have been a lad of few words, but his advice of "two balls left" was right on the money; the putt had curled exactly that much.

Max managed to get off the second and third tees better than he had the first. Chip's comment, "You *can* hit it," delivered with a grin, showed that the lad was warming up to Max. Having hit those two greens in regulation, he went on to the fourth hole at even par.

"Go for it," advised Chip. When Max asked what he meant, the boy merely nodded in the direction of the trees that guarded the turn of the dogleg to the left. Max checked the scorecard, the map of the hole, and the wind. It looked like the smart thing to do on this par-4 hole was to lay a three-iron straight out to the turn. He turned to Chip to ask for that club. He handed Max his driver and nodded toward the trees again. Yes, he could hit a high draw just right of the tallest tree and, hopefully, over the others. His resultant pitch-and-run shot from the apron of the green led to a tap-in birdie.

With his two playing partners standing at one-over and two-over respectively, Max felt pretty good about himself as he walked to the fifth tee. But he thought of what he knew about flow states and playing golf, or any sport, "in the zone." He could allow himself idle, analytical, off-task thoughts in between shots. But his best chance of achieving the optimal mental state, and to keep his good round going, was to minimize any social comparisons and score-keeping. He used self-talk to guide himself through his pre-shot routine, not only on that tee shot, but before every shot and putt he executed that day. He expressed emotions in a low-key manner, and only briefly, after any good or bad shot. Because Chip kept his comments short, to the point, and unobtrusive, Max was able to shift from them into hitting mode with little or no effort.

Time flew by. It seemed to be only a matter of an hour before Max was on the eighteenth fairway and realized that he stood at four under par for the round. Drat! Self-distraction had now reared its ugly head; nervousness could not be far behind. He took two deep breaths, sighing forcefully each time, and stood frozen by his ball in the fairway. Chip came to the rescue. He interrupted Max's reverie by handing him his six-iron. His quick nod and wink snapped Max into his routine of visualizing the flight of his next shot toward the flag, addressing the ball in a well-balanced manner, feeling himself project the ball onto its path, and then letting it happen. Max disappointingly left the resulting twelve-foot putt a couple of inches short, but he felt grateful for the easy tap-in for par to end the round.

Max could finally permit himself to leave his mental cocoon and attend to others. He asked each playing partner what he had shot, and thanked them for their good company. They congratulated him. Then Max discovered that they had good cause for doing so. The scoreboard revealed that his sixty-eight was the lowest round of the day thus far. And when the final players had had their scores posted, Max was the winner by two shots.

"Go buy yourself a new wedge," Max advised Chip as he slipped him a four-hundred-dollar tip. "See you here next year?" First wide-eyed at the cash in his hand, then giving Max his only broad smile of the day, Chip simply nodded.

Back in his apartment by 7:15 that Sunday, Max wondered aloud, "Whom should I call first?" She answered after the first ring.

"Hello."

"Good evening, Mademoiselle," Max started in his best impression of a snooty English butler. "This is Parsimony Rumpbottom, and I represent the insurance company of Disquietude, Dismemberment, and Death. That's 3-D for short. The reason for my call this evening—and I trust that I am not disturbing you—is to inform you of our new whole life policy." Max couldn't read her silence. Was she busy stifling a laugh? Was she about to hang up? Did he finally have her duped? "With the chance to save for retirement while guarding against the unfortunate possibility of decapitation, this 3-D opportunity is too good to miss. Miss? Are you there, Miss?"

"Aaaaaahhhhhh!" Her scream made Max pull the telephone away from his ear.

"Hello? Mel—I mean Mademoiselle?" he asked with a mix of regular and character voices.

A guttural tone, with a trace of feminine quality, simply said, "I'm afraid you're too late, buddy." And she hung up.

That was fun, Max thought. He redialed.

After four rings, the familiar voice answered, "Hello, Max."

"Yes, Mel, it is I. Guess what?"

"You lost the tournament and your mind in one fell swoop?" she ventured.

"Right on one count. But I now have a small wad of money, some of which I'd like to spend before it gets to the bank."

"You won?" Max enjoyed the tone of excitement in her voice.

"That I did. If you've got the time this evening, I'd be glad to take you out to tell you all about it."

"Where shall we go? How soon will you pick me up?"

"I feel like visiting Taco's Tostadas. It's a cozy place in which to munch some tortilla chips and word salad. I could probably be at your place by 8:00."

"My dismembered body and I will be expecting you."

Max telephoned Mom and Dad.

When his mother answered, Max jumped right in with the news: "You are now speaking with the winner of The Club Special—"

"Oh, that's great news! Hold on, let me get your father to the other phone."

He came on with, "You won? First place?"

"You bet," Max beamed. "I'm three thousand six hundred dollars richer. And you feared that I would never amount to anything."

"Way to go, Son. And it's none too early, and certainly not too late, to begin paying us back for all the money we spent on your college education, not to mention those golf lessons we bought you as a kid."

He's still quick on the uptake, thought Max. There's no way that premature dementia was taking hold of Dad. Mom was sharp, too.

"I'm proud of you, Son," added Mom. "And Dad's right. Even though we enjoy it here in Florida, we wouldn't mind your paying to send us to Barbados for a week or two."

"Gee, and I thought that maybe, just maybe, you'd like me to use some of the prize money to get down to see you."

"Yes, that would be nice, dear. In Barbados."

Dad got serious. "How did you do it? What did you shoot?"

"I kept the ball out of the trees, had a couple of good sand saves, and took only twenty-nine putts to carve out a sixty-eight."

"Whew, you were hot."

"I had a young, helpful caddy but mainly, Dad, it was the cross-handed putting. I had a good feeling about my change to it last year, and it's starting to pay off. I know that you think it's crazy—"

"How much did you say you won today?" Dad interrupted. "Four thousand dollars? That could buy my silence on the matter of your weird putting style."

"I'll buy you dinner when I see you. Is that good enough?"

"It's a deal," replied Mom and Dad.

Who else would share his good feeling about his victory, thought Max. He telephoned his sister.

After four rings, a young girl's high-pitched voice answered, "Hel-lo?" Rather than open a conversation with his niece, who might feel intimidated because she might not remember him well, he expressed the routine, "May I please speak with your mother?"

"Hello?" Like her daughter, Ruth also answered the telephone with a questioning inflection.

"Ms. Azure?" His sister had declined to take her husband's last name in wedlock, citing her professional publications as the reason.

"Yes." Was it reluctance or impatience that he detected in her tone?

"This is Agent Arrow of the Internal Retinue Service," Max stated in a deep and slow, but mildly slurred, voice. "The IRS has received a report that your servants have been doing a commendable job of meeting your every need, including the little whims to which you are prone. I am calling simply to follow up on their report in order to ensure that you are satisfied with the retinue service, internally and with feeling, as it is currently being provided."

"Let me guess, Max. One of those stray golf shots I've been reading about finally found its way to your noggin."

"Well, I'm feeling a little light-headed, if that's what you mean," said Max in his normal tone of voice.

"Is it good news? Is that why you've called?" Her voice sounded better now, more relaxed but maybe a tad sarcastic. Her sense of humor wasn't what it used to be.

"As a matter of fact, Sis, I just thought you might like to bask in the reflected glory of the new club professional champion of New York State."

"Way to go, Bro! Congratulations!" Her kudos were sincere, Max could tell, but her brevity suggested that she was distracted. Sure enough, he heard a shriek in the background.

"Quiet, girls, I'm on the phone," Ruth hissed. "So, Max, that's nice. Really. I'm proud of you."

"Yeah, I thought it was a good occasion to call, an upbeat one, you know, and a chance to check on how you are doing."

"I'd like to talk for a while, Max, but the girls' dinner is cooking, they're playing too roughly again, their father plans to be home late from work, and I have a project to get to work on if these two little angels of mine ever wind down enough to go to bed."

"Busy, busy, as usual," commented Max, the wind out of his sails.

"Yes, we are. I'm doing swell, Max. So are the girls and my husband. It's just that, sometimes, I'd like to step off the treadmill of life for a respite."

"Uh huh. Stress rears its ugly head in all walks, and stages, of life."

"Yes, but listen. We really are planning to fly back East for a visit, hopefully next summer. We want to see you. Holy cannoli, I doubt that the girls would even recognize their Uncle Max 'cause it's been so long."

They continued their small talk for only a couple more minutes before disconnecting with the mutual promise to stay in touch more often. He knew that Ruth's plate was full, with family and household responsibilities on top of her job as assistant professor of sociology at UCSB. Nevertheless, Max missed the deeper conversations he used to share with his older sister, when their early years of sibling rivalry had been replaced by several years of adolescent closeness.

"Oooh, you have such nice, strong hands," cooed Melody as Max massaged her back.

"I need them to knead you," he responded. Actually, he was using a combination of stroking and pushing with direct pressure.

"Did you say you learned how to do this in aikido class? All I've ever seen you do there is throw one another around."

"Kiatsu, which is akin to acupressure, is not exactly a 'demonstration' sport," Max said. "We save it for times when spectators are not around."

"And do you pair up with any of the females in the class for this sort of thing?" she asked with a hint of jealousy.

"Yes, indeed. But only you get the bare skin treatment." Max directed the tips of his thumbs into the firm muscles just on both sides of Melody's spine, halfway down her back. She tensed briefly as he hit a sensitive spot, so he let up slightly as she breathed deeply. He felt muscles soften as she sighed. She lay silently, following Max's advice to keep breathing deeply and steadily, as he applied his thumbs to some other typical tight spots near her scapulae, shoulders, and neck.

Max paused. "Now, phase two of this massage requires a bit of lubricant—would you care for the hazelnut lotion or a bit of almond oil?"

"Ooh, you choose. You're the one who will smell the scent. I get the good feeling."

Max proceeded to use some long strokes down and across her back, shoulders, and arms. He used more pressure with his thumbs alongside her spine, this time with their sliding gradually along their slippery paths. He gave some extra attention to her trapezius muscles, those reservoirs of tension near the top of the back. As he carried out this concerted, tender act of giving to Melody, feeling pangs of arousal in the process, Max could feel her relaxing under his touch. Did he want to ease her into slumber, or did he have a more passionate conclusion to their massage session in mind? Perhaps Melody picked up on his mixture of moods.

"This is wonderful, Max. But I think that the tournament winner, the new champion club pro of the state, deserves some similar attention."

"If you insist," he assented.

A delicate balance of arousal and relaxation, ebbing and flowing in both of them, lasted into the early morning hours. They exchanged massages seamlessly, their hands roaming and soothing first their backs, then their fronts, from their uppermost to their lowermost anatomical regions. Erotic energies eventually took over as they wholly explored one another's erogenous zones, reveling in their level of intimacy. Their give and take were genuinely mutual. Max truly felt like a winner that glorious Sunday.

Sunday to Monday went from exalted to exhausted. In his state of satisfied fatigue, Max was not ready for the sobering news stories that unfolded that day. First came word of the death of another member of the clergy, a Hindu swami, the day before, at a nearby golf course, no less. It was a double-header because a Protestant cleric, Reverend Martin Eagleton, was killed on a golf course near Buffalo. About two hours later, none other than Melody reported from on location at a course near Batavia that an elder of the Church of Jesus Christ and Latter-Day Saints had been struck, and nearly killed, by a golf ball. By the time the dinner hour approached, the board of directors of Max's golf course had declared it closed until further notice.

Until then, the police had been trying to play things cagey, and the media had cooperated, agreeing to limit its conjecture to the occasional editorial or side story. Now, all heck broke loose. Tales of terrorism sprang from the lips of television interviewees and the pens of newspaper columnists, not only locally but from coast to coast. Online bloggers fanned the flames of fear. The term "serial killing" had been bantered about previously, but it appeared full-blown as a well-promulgated headline that evening. Hypotheses to account for the rash of attacks ranged from profiles of the type of teenagers who might be willing to act out their youthful rage, to a conspiracy of expert golfers whose psyches had run amok, to various terrorist groups that could have the motive and means to embark upon this swath of aggression. The media stirred up public fear of Satanic cults, inadvertently making vulnerable, troubled adolescents curious to learn more about them.

Max shook his head in response to each story that blossomed. He surely did not know which theory to believe. He hung and shook his head despondently in response to the way people were reacting to events. Max could understand the sense of crisis, but given his bias, he felt that the precautionary closing of his golf course and others, not just to clergy but to everyone, was overkill.

Claude and his cohorts liked the notoriety, even in its indirect form. He had mixed feelings about the closing of many regional golf courses. On the one hand, it met one of the stated goals of the group. It de-popularized the repugnant sport and kept the religious leaders away from their sacrilegious pastime. On the other hand, his aim went well beyond the discouragement of clergy from playing golf. The targets of his crusade were now much less vulnerable to the members of his group, both emotionally and physically. He would have to find a way to shift the motivations of HH into high gear in a new direction.

Then events dictated Claude's new thrust.

As the week progressed, first one and then another terrorist cult took credit for the killings. An American separatist group, one with the desire to go back to the laws and freedoms of Revolutionary War times, reported by letter to a newspaper that some of its members had taken matters into their own hands. Frustrated by what they perceived as governmental persecution that infringed on their rights to hunt, shoot, and use weapons as they saw fit, they had launched into the series of attacks. The other self-proclaimed culprit was a branch of an Islamic jihadist group abroad. Its stated aim was to avenge the sins of the Judeo-Christian tradition against the righteous followers of Allah and his prophet, Muhammad.

Claude felt insulted. What blasphemy! How dare others, in the names of their unjust causes, claim credit for his murderous masterpiece? He considered that he, too, should submit some sort of press release in order to set the country straight. Not only could it do no harm since he would send it to the press in an untraceable way, but it might help his organization grow. He felt sure that thousands, even millions, of Americans felt as he did. Maybe it was time to present them with the correct thinking about the state of the nation. He could paint a picture of the wicked world that would show people not only the error of their ways but also his righteous path to redemption.

Claude's feeling of insult escalated into outrage the following day. He considered the closing of golf courses to be a mixed blessing, and the false claiming of credit for the clergy cleansing by rival factions to be irritating and unjust. But he felt unequivocally disgusted when he read the announcement in *The Buffalo Blurb* that the parishioners of the late Reverend Eagleton were planning a charity golf tournament in his honor. Ignoring the connections between golf and the reverend's premature demise, his followers wanted to bring together local clergy and public figures at a fundraising event. Claude immediately sat down to draft a press release that would not only set the record straight but also point the heathens of the world in the right direction, toward Holy Help. It also dawned on him that the charity golf tournament, brimming with reporters and Reverend Eagleton's fellow clergymen, might provide a well-publicized opportunity to carry out one or more of HH's divine interventions.

IX

CLIENTELE

"I STARTED SEEING AN INTERESTING NEW CLIENT TODAY," confided Mitch. "It's a ten-year-old boy who still soils himself on occasion, seemingly without any physical reason for doing so." He leaned forward on the bar, shook his head and squinted his eyes as though in pain, then sighed and took a sip of his beer.

"What kind of a look is that?" Max inquired. "Are you disgusted that the kid messes his pants? You look like it's more than that."

"I think it's a lot more than that, and I smell something rotten."

"Besides the boy?"

"Yes, smart guy, besides the boy. The youngster clearly has that problem, encopresis, but his parents tell me that he has other problems. I mean, they make him sound like the most devilish, bedeviled child ever born."

"Like how?"

"Well, for example, they claim that he has ADHD—Attention-Deficit/Hyperactivity Disorder—and can neither sit still nor concentrate on anything, anywhere, for more than a few seconds. They state that he is depressed, obsessive-compulsive, and learning disabled as well. They report that he bullies his younger sister and most of the children in the neighborhood. He's a picky eater whose sleep habits are even worse than his appetite. He lies pathologically. He's scared of everything—strangers, dogs, bugs, the dark, heights, you name it—yet often goes where he does not belong."

"He sounds like a tough case!" Max looked at Mitch with wide-eyed concern.

"Yes, I guess he is. But the rub is that I don't see such problems in the kid—at least not yet. I know that I only just met him, but the boy showed me good manners and positive self-control. He remained seated and focused, both while talking with me and while doing a drawing of a person. He was able to read the cards of a game, and he readily played by the rules. It just struck me that his parents might be exaggerating his problems, big time. It also bothered me that they wanted to run through his problems, and label them psychiatrically, right in front of their son."

"You don't want him to hear about himself?"

"I don't want him to hear how badly significant others think of him. Self-fulfilling prophecies and expectancy effects can be mighty powerful."

"It sounds as though his parents 'help' him to feel crappy and unhappy." Max sipped his own brew. "So, what's your game plan, Coach?"

"I had the parents sign request of information forms to send to the boy's school and pediatrician. I'm curious to hear what others think of him. If my hunch is correct, he could be a victim of Factitious Disorder Imposed on Another, also known as Munchausen Syndrome."

"I beg your pardon," Max commented, genuinely puzzled.

"I suspect that the boy is less disturbed than his parents report. The bulk of the problem could be theirs. They might have a need, or indeed a disorder, that causes them to overstate what is wrong with their son. By doing so, they get to look and act like saints who are seeking the best of care for their offspring. They attract lots of caring concern from others, which makes them feel virtuous, and they get secondary gain from the martyrdom of tolerating their difficult son. Meanwhile, they conveniently scapegoat him for whatever happens to cause them stress in their personal, family, and professional lives."

"Goodness gracious!" reacted Max. "They'd do that to their own son?"

"Yes, and maybe even with good intentions. That's the paradoxical nature of the disorder; the problem is theirs, not the boy's."

"Ugh," Max empathized.

"Yeah, ugh. Trying to change parental perceptions in a case like that can get ugly."

They lifted their pint glasses and drank simultaneously.

Mitch got mixed responses to his inquiries about his new young client, Ned. The pediatrician, Dr. Gibbon Schotz, tended to confirm parental concerns and even offer diagnostic labels based on their complaints. But he wasn't sure himself, having based his impressions mainly on parental input, so he referred the boy to the school psychologist who, in turn, referred him to Mitch. The report from the school psychologist, Ms. Binet Wechsler, largely upheld Mitch's suspicions. Ned had periodically displayed incontinence throughout his school history but otherwise functioned pretty well. Ms. Wechsler had failed to find empirical or anecdotal evidence of a learning disability, or signs of an attentional disorder, in Ned. He managed to get mediocre grades in his regular fifth-grade class, though his participation in physical education class was sometimes compromised by his odorous "condition." His social life was a dud. Peers kept their distance from him. Ms. Wechsler wasn't sure if Ned's lack of enrollment in any extracurricular activities was his own or his parents' choosing.

Mitch felt grateful for the information, and for the newest of many interesting clients he had. But his eyes instinctively sank downward and he shook his head sadly, lamenting that this problem was too common. It troubled him to think back on several other cases of Factitious Disorder Imposed on Another that he had encountered. The parents did not want to, or could not, hear about the assets of their child. Mitch had helped one such family attain some stability, but the others were stuck in dysfunctionality; the parents simply took their victimized child to another healthcare professional who was more willing to share their negative perspective. Ned's family could be another tough nut to crack.

Sam Sneadeker, the head professional at Bent Grass Golf Links, did not recognize the two men in his pro shop. And he thought it odd that they wore button-down shirts, unusually constrictive clothing for golfers. But Sam didn't mind their taking their time sampling the putters he had on display. With a rush of golfers arriving to sign in before the Thursday night league was scheduled to tee off, Sam was busy enough to give the strangers no more thought. He might have considered it odd, but did not notice, when the two hung around the putting green for the better part of an hour, mainly standing and watching the coming and going of various golfers without doing much practice putting of their own. When they reentered the shop, again taking their time perusing the merchandise, Sam remained too occupied to care much about them. He was downright grateful when each of them paid cash for two sleeves of balls, even though it was irritating that they took fifteen minutes to decide which brands to purchase. Their choice of Surefire XDs and Whizbang 90s suggested that they were either shopping for a good golfer or were advanced players themselves.

Bart and Ernie had become pretty adept at scouting the lay of the land, and identifying religious patrons, at various golf courses. While the staff in the pro shop busied themselves with other customers, they discreetly eyed the sign-in sheet and tried to match golfers with their names. They stepped outside at times to finish the process of identification, jotting down a few notes along the way. Only when back in the car, and after driving to a pull-off from the road out of sight of the pro shop, did they compare names of patrons with the list of clergy members from the online yellow pages of the local telephone book. Their final preparatory maneuver was to cruise around the perimeter of the golf property while examining the map provided on the scorecard.

On Friday morning, Priscilla telephoned Mitch's office to discuss details of their plan to go horseback riding the following morning. She hoped that he hadn't forgotten and planned to play golf instead. To her dismay, his voicemail message came on:

"Most of the people who call me hang up;

They hate to talk to a machine.

But listen now, person, whoever you are,

In this there is nothing obscene.

I'm not to blame if I'm at work or at play;

I *need* electronic assistance.

So please leave a message as short as you like,

And please minimize your resistance."

"Better, Mitch, that's better. That greeting is reasonable compared to your others. It's just after 8:00 now. I'll be heading into the law office shortly. Call me here at home soon, or at work later, so we can finish planning our trip to the stables tomorrow. Ta-ta." Priscilla decided to try Mitch at home too, just in case he was slow to get into his office today.

"Aikido and psychology

Are just what they're cracked up to be.

They often keep Mitch busily

Away from this phone, don't you see?

So, if you have some words for me,

Please leave them now, recordedly."

"Holy hitch, your messages make me twitch, Mitch. There. I said a rhyme. How'd I do, pardner? This message is the same as the one that I just left at your office. It's just after eight. Call me."

Mitch missed Priscilla's calls because he was engrossed in another fun-filled early morning session with one of his favorite, and longest-standing, clients, Simon. Mr. Clothymik liked to rearrange their meeting times, depending on his moods.

"Hi, Si." Simon preferred the shortened version of his name. "How are things going with you?"

"Up and down, as usual," said the stocky, balding forty-something man wearing a leisure suit. "You win some and you lose some."

"Please be more specific," Mitch encouraged with a grin, expecting the usually effervescent Mr. Clothymik to respond in a spirited manner.

"First of all, thank God I'm not religious."

"Oh?"

"Well, not only are all those priests and ministers getting knocked off by some cuckoo homicidal maniacs, but my wife wants me to join her new church and go to services and meetings four times per week."

"And you don't share her faith?" inquired Mitch.

"Faith schmaith, she goes for the cookies and conversation. The godforsaken religious zealots there tell her not only what a wonderful person she is, but also how she could unload any and all miseries by listening to their gospel. Then they assign her all sorts of stuff to read. Can you imagine—they even give homework? And she does it! And she wants me to do it too!" Si looked at Mitch with his wide brown eyes searching for empathy.

"Help me get my bearings here, Si, by answering a couple of questions."

"Okay, shoot!"

"What religion, if any, are you?"

"I was raised Jewish. I had a Bar Mitzvah, and did a good job of it too. Then I went to college and lost the faith. I took a couple of courses in Buddhism. It seemed much more real and down to Earth. It was around that time that I coined the phrase, 'I shoulda been a Buddha, and I woulda if I coulda.' I meditated for a while, but college life being what it was, I medicated quite a bit, too, if you catch my drift."

"Yes, so . . . ?"

"So I entered the mainstream of life as a Jewish Buddhist agnostic—holding some old beliefs along with some new, but practicing nothing. My wife seemed to feel the same, at least when we met and eventually wed, but recently she got sucked into that new religion by one of her friends."

"So, you're glad that you're not religious because you feel upset by your wife's involvement in her new faith?"

"Wouldn't you be? She's out three evenings and half of Sunday! Holy schmoly, how much religion do you need? Is life with me that bad that she's gotta go looking for God to help her out?"

"You feel really annoyed about this." Mitch watched as his comment, or merely the passage of time and energy, caused much of the agitation to drain from Si's demeanor. He sank back into his chair and sighed.

"I'm going nowhere. I know that."

Mitch's thinking flashed to the episodes of depression that he himself had experienced over the years. The week-long blues through which he had suffered during graduate school, unable to get out of bed to attend any of his classes, had fueled Mitch's empathy for clients like Si. "You're putting yourself down, Si. I thought that things are okay with you, at least on the surface. But you may not feel that way."

"I'm alive and kicking. My job is secure—but boring. I'm an adequate husband and father—but my wife is building this religious wall between us, and our son and daughter cling to their own ways rather than talking to me about anything. I'm doing nothing meaningful with my life. It's just passing along with, as I've said, ups and downs, with nothing to be proud of."

"I may be off-base here, Si, but it sounds like you're describing your own spiritual crisis. It may not be a specific religion, such as your wife's, that you desire, but you seem to feel discontent because you don't know just how you fit into the cosmos. You're suffering from the holy doldrums. You have no spiritual path of your own."

"Yes, that could be. I remember feeling that the Buddhist teachings really make sense for me. But I studied them so many years ago that I feel totally out of touch."

When he was feeling melancholic, Simon was much easier to calm down and focus, thought Mitch. His symptoms of bipolar disorder—

mania and depression—were relatively mild and did not debilitate Si too drastically in his everyday life. But his discontent was persistent; dietary changes, exercise, and counseling had yet to eradicate his alternating episodes of self-confidence and self-effacement. He was reluctant to venture into taking medication to reduce his mood swings, and Mitch tended to respect that stance. Perhaps an injection of spirituality could be beneficial.

"Do you still have your books about Buddhism? If you coulda been a Buddha, then maybe you shoulda."

Si chuckled, nodded, and visibly started to rise above his brief episode of the blues. "Yes, and I might even glance at my Hebrew prayer book and a couple of other books about Judaism. I'm not ready to give up my hobbies for religion, mind you."

"No, of course not."

"But it wouldn't hurt to read up on some of that religious malarkey."

"However you want to phrase it is okay by me."

Mitch helped Si work out the details of his homework, suggested the modern Buddhist magazine *Lion's Roar*, and explored some vehicles for better marital interaction before calling it a session.

Max was grateful that the management of Rolling Greens had seen fit to keep the practice facilities and pro shop open during the temporary closure of most golf courses in the region. His meager salary was supplemented by a commission on pro shop sales, now reduced by the limited flow of traffic to the club, and by his lesson fees. Not only did he need the cash; he also needed the practice site at which to tune his game for the upcoming U.S. Open Qualifier, just one week away.

That Friday, in late May, Max was slated to start his day with an eager new student. He liked giving lessons to children. Most of them were intent on learning, impressed with Max's golfing skills, and respectful of his teachings. Then there was Roger.

Roger was nine years old and already knew it all. Describing himself as a "tweenager," the freckle-faced lad with strawberry blond hair stood several inches under five feet tall. He looked at his father with resentment when delivered for his first lesson that day, and he gave Max a dirty look that spelled uncooperative behavior from the get-go. He probably viewed the pro as a usurper of his precious recreational time, so he soon sought to shape their lesson time to suit himself.

"Hi, Roger," Max greeted, "and welcome to Rolling Greens."

"Where are the golf balls? Dad said I was coming here to hit golf balls."

"Yes, we'll be heading out to the driving range in just a minute."

"Dad, this is boring. Can we go home now? Or let's just play the course."

Mr. Dodge spoke patiently to his son, though Max caught slight irritation in his eyes. "You're here to take a lesson from Mr. Azure so that you can learn to play the game better and enjoy it more. So, please do your best at whatever this fine golf professional asks you to do."

Max picked up his cue swiftly. "Grab your clubs and follow me, Roger."

The boy dragged his golf bag to the lesson tee. "Oh, there's a bunch of balls," he said when he spotted the bucket Max had ready and waiting.

"I understand that you've played before, Roger. Let me see you hit a couple of seven-iron shots."

Roger wanted to grip a club any old way and simply take a mighty rip at the golf ball. His first swing would have hit Max if he hadn't backed up reflexively from the boy's baseball-plane wind-up. "Shoot!" Roger exclaimed as he whiffed. Max looked up to see his father's reaction to the wild swing but saw only Mr. Dodge's retreating back as he headed to the putting green. Max was on his own.

"Whoa, horsey. Let's bring that swing down to Earth."

Roger wasn't waiting for any directions. And he managed to wallop the ball the second time. It zinged almost dead right off the hosel of the club, the shanked shot missing Max's leg by only inches.

"Roger, please hold on for a minute. A good golf shot needs a bunch of parts: a proper grip, balanced stance, smooth backswing, and well-timed swing at the ball."

Before Max could finish that sentence, or intervene, Roger had poked another ball from the bucket onto the ground and taken a swipe at it. At least he was no longer swinging too high, above the ball. This time, his club dug deep into the turf.

He said, "These are lousy golf balls. And don't you have a mat I could hit from?"

"Roger, please put down the club for a minute," Max requested. Roger poked into the now-spilled bucket to nudge another ball near him. "Holy Artful Dodger! Drop the club, Roger!" Max commanded with twice his normal volume. As an aikidoist and golf pro, Max always tried to keep his cool. But Roger needed some direct harmonizing with his impulsive, unruly nature. Indeed, he complied.

"Driver now?" he inquired.

"No!" Max snapped, then sighed. With his equanimity partially restored, Max decided to try what Dr. Mitch would call "self-disclosure." "Let me hit one or two, just to give you a different perspective, a look at another way to hit a ball." Instead of trying passively to watch and instruct Roger in action, Max gave modeling a try.

Picking up Roger's seven-iron, and directing him out of harm's way, Max effortlessly stroked a ball out toward the center green of the practice range. He glanced at Roger. Max had gotten his attention. He hit another shot precisely to the same location. "See how I do it? Can you tell me any differences between my shots and yours?"

"Yeah, you got lucky. Let me do it again."

Yessiree—in Roger, egocentricity knew no bounds. It took a while for Max to gain control of the lesson. And Roger, perhaps due to his unrestrained ferocity, managed to hit some pretty long shots. Some golf teachers preach that youngsters should be encouraged to swing with all their might, with distance as the first goal and direction as a later one.

Rambunctious Roger surely had the prerequisite skill and temperament to carry out that lesson plan!

Max was relieved to have Larry Bogart approach the lesson tee after Roger. Bogey did not always exhibit perfect manners, with flashes of temper evident just beneath the surface when shots were not going his way, but he loved golf and was eager to improve with the aid of lessons. He greeted Max with, "Hey, Coach, how ya' doin' today?"

"Better now, Bogey, and thanks for asking."

"Having some rough times on the tee?" inquired Larry.

"Nothing I can't handle; it's nice to have you here for a change of pace. By the way, what do you do for a living?" asked Max, voicing a query that he'd entertained for a while. Bogey seemed to be available to play golf more than the average guy his age.

"Well, a little like you, I'm a teacher. I teach industrial arts at a community college."

"Since I see you here at the club with some regularity, is it safe to assume that you teach part-time, or perhaps evenings?"

"Right on both counts. And what counts right now is how many strokes I've been taking to reach the greens. My putting has gotten a little better since our last lesson, but I've had to aim for double bogeys lately."

Bogey's set-up and alignment had slipped off-kilter, Max soon detected. It took only a little adjustment for him to hit some straight, solid shots—at least on the practice range.

Big Wayne Windham was Max's next lesson of the day. Like Bogey, he was a welcome regular with an avid, though errant, approach to the game of golf. Max could get him to line up properly; however, Wayne's large turn, lurch forward, and resultant head movement made his initial alignment moot. His moving center of balance sent shots every which way. Max repeated the lessons on centering and balance, culled from aikido as well as golf, and saw Wayne settle into a steadier swing.

"Thanks, Max. I needed that," expressed the big lug. Max silently said to himself that he needed that, a sense of successful instruction.

Mr. and Mrs. Smith brought JD to Mitch's office, and right on time. After his having missed two sessions, they had caught on that maybe he couldn't be trusted to get there after school on his own. They had asked him pointblank whether he liked Dr. Treasure and wanted to meet with him anymore, and he had replied in the affirmative. Indeed, Mitch witnessed JD's sheepish, guilty look when he entered the office.

"Sorry I missed my last two appointments, Dr. Treasure. I had somewhere else I had to be."

"Well, I'm glad that you're here now. May I ask where it was that you 'had to be' instead of here?"

"You may ask, but I can't say. It's a secret."

"Okeydokey, if that's how it has to be."

"Okeydokey, Doc? Isn't that expression a little out of touch with the times?"

"Right on, Daddy-O, if you say so."

"Have you been dipping into your clients' medications again, Dr. T?"

"I'm just high on life, JD," Mitch explained, now satisfied that rapport with JD was back on track. "But that's enough banter about linguistics. Today I'd like us to talk about . . ."

Their session followed Mitch's agenda well, though JD occasionally seemed preoccupied with something on his mind. Mitch had to repeat himself a few times and work to maintain eye contact. Mitch chalked up the distractible behavior to JD's ongoing depression and his reluctance to hear the feedback, both good and bad, that Mitch had recently received about his progress in school. Still, disrupting classroom proceedings for attention but considerably less often than previously, JD was letting his homework production slide toward nothing.

Mitch asked, "How are you spending time outside class these days? Are you hanging with Mike? Your guidance counselor reports that you guys have become buddies in class."

JD glanced up from his trance at the sound of Mike's name. "Yeah, I hang out with Mike sometimes, but mostly with other friends."

Mitch wasn't sure about the veracity of that statement because, according to parents and school staff, JD had no other friends. Mitch released JD from therapeutic bondage ten minutes early in order to chat with Mr. and Mrs. Smith. They declared that JD had, indeed, spoken lately of hanging with new friends, but they had gotten no names from him. They had been pleased to see a spark in JD after his first few sessions with Mitch, but he had since regressed. Mitch took a fresh tack.

"When was JD happiest? Think back through his life, and tell me what he was doing when he seemed to be functioning well and/or feeling content."

"Gee, that's a tough one," responded Mr. Smith. His wife simply nodded, and they both screwed up their faces and looked aside in pursuit of their memories.

Mrs. Smith spoke first. "He liked birthday parties, being the center of attention and getting to rip open presents. And he has always gotten along well with our dog, Mittens."

"Well, the party thing is understandable," analyzed Mitch. "I like your report that he's been good to the dog—that's definitely a positive attribute." He added it to his notes about JD.

"You know, I was wary of taking him along, but JD always seemed to enjoy going golfing with me," piped in Mr. Smith.

"Golfing?!" Mitch nearly choked on the word.

"Yes. You might have thought that he'd be so distracted and make such a racket that he'd be a real nuisance. But he walked along pretty well—you know, kept up with me and stayed out of danger—and he even hit some nice shots when I gave him the chance."

"When was this?" inquired Mitch. "How old was he?"

"Oh, he must have been seven or eight. My sacroiliac didn't like the game nearly as well as the rest of me did, so I had to give it up at that time. Come to think of it, he asked me to take him several times after that, didn't he, Honey?"

"Yes," replied Mrs. Smith. "I remember thinking how odd it was for him to like golf, of all things."

At the same time that Mitch was learning about JD's connection to golf, Max was still connecting with Wayne and his wayward swing. Sometimes Max felt that he'd already said it all and that it was up to the student to practice and progress. Max had pointed the way, and Wayne knew what to do; now it was up to him and whatever level of talent he had to make straighter shots a habit. Of course, he could also show and teach him how to curve the ball a bit. And so he did. And Wayne responded with a pull hook instead of a draw and a slice instead of a fade. Let the lessons continue.

Next on the practice tee came Sister Rotini, wary of the new hazards faced by certain unfortunate, golfing members of the clergy but still eager to resume the sport to the best of her ability when the coast was clear. Eleanor Wholesome followed her, engaging Max in their shared local knowledge of their golf course and its members while simultaneously helping to keep Max financially solvent. She was her usual pleasant and accurate self on the lesson tee.

JD made even more new friends on Saturday. The HH meeting attracted a new high of nineteen guys, many of whom had exited special education such as the program in which JD was enrolled, and all of whom felt disgruntled about their lives. Claude raised their hopes by acknowledging their suffering, identifying some sources of it, and promising deliverance.

X

THICKENING CLOUDS

THE PRESS RELEASE FROM HOLY HELP reached the Buffalo and Rochester newspapers on Monday, shortly *before* word from police that another golf course killing had occurred. This time, the untimely death was near Erie, Pennsylvania. The victim was Rabbi Klubman, leader of a reform synagogue who received a "True Shot" golf ball to the temple while he was playing the seventh hole at the Rough Fairways Golf Club northeast of the city. The course was uncrowded, as was typical of Monday mornings, and the rabbi's playing partner, Arthur O'Bounds, was too busy searching the woods for his errant shot to have witnessed the crime.

As for the press release, it consisted of a brief, boastful claim of credit for the series of golf course executions, followed by a lengthy diatribe against modern society. No one specifically was blamed for creating the misguided path they accused humans of treading, but clergy were scapegoated for perpetuation of the sinful, decadent, greedy, sacrilegious lives of most Americans. Injustices against the downtrodden and misused proletariat were blamed on a conspiratorial conglomerate of political, industrial, and religious factions. The last two paragraphs of the manifesto foretold the coming of salvation for humankind by the Almighty Lord through the hand of Holy Help. It appealed to the God-fearing people of the country to see the error of their ways, renounce their current religious and political leadership, and devote themselves to the righteous path of HH. It ended with the promise of more information forthcoming about the HH movement.

Neither local nor federal law enforcement agencies had any record of an organization calling itself Holy Help or going by the initials HH. They did, however, have some open files on religious zealots who were believed to be living in the Western or Central New York area, so their research started with background checks of them. Furthermore, they scrutinized the style of writing of the manifesto in order to hypothesize the educational level, intelligence, and cultural background of its author(s). Federal agents analyzed the document for signs of any regional dialects that could begin to narrow down the author's geographical origin. The computer-printed press release offered no opportunity for handwriting analysis, but the document was submitted to a crime lab to try to determine the type, brand, and age of the printer and computer on which it was generated. The paper was analyzed for its content, age, manufacturer, and brand name.

The pursuit of evidence and suspects was going to take time, despite the considerable manpower devoted to the case by law enforcement officials at all levels. In the meantime, police patrol officers were alerted to be on the lookout for signs of any suspicious gatherings of people. They reviewed the sales records of many hardware and gun stores, seeking to uncover the components of the murder weapon and to trace their purchaser. Much time had already been devoted to detecting the type of weapon that was being used to propel golf balls with deadly force, but munitions experts could not figure out how one might construct a portable golf ball bazooka in the absence of a loud explosive charge to shoot it. All they could surmise was that the culprits possessed specific technological expertise in addition to a bizarre religious agenda.

Maybe some golf courses in New York and Pennsylvania would play it safe by closing, but most chose instead to remain open with the addition of security measures—hiring additional golf course rangers to roll around in their golf carts looking for any suspicious happenings—and cautionary warnings. Golf courses are big business; they had profits to earn. Besides, it appeared that only clergymen, not the general public, incurred any risk by playing the game. When Rolling Greens reopened, Max was glad to be able to expand his game from the practice tee back to the full golf course.

No matter what was happening in the local vicinity, the U.S. Open was scheduled to be played as planned in a few short weeks. After four previous disappointments, Max felt determined to qualify for the big event.

Birdies' Brook Golf Club had been well chosen for the regional qualifying round for the U.S. Open. Like most Open courses, the place was lavishly maintained. Its weed-free fairways felt like plush carpet and set up the ball nicely. The greens were good at holding incoming shots. At the same time, however, the dense rough could grab a clubhead and force a feeble shot. Plenty of trees guarded the fairways, and bunkers abounded around the fast-rolling greens. Uneven lies were the rule rather than the exception. Before his practice round, Max relearned from the host professional what Mitch had already told him—that the name of the course had been based as much on the nearby museum of a famous avian artist and naturalist, Roger Tory Peterson, as on the goal of the golfers there. Birds were much more common in the local trees than on the players' scorecards.

The day of the qualifying round that Saturday dawned sunny and seasonably warm. Dressed conservatively, in navy blue trousers and royal blue golf shirt, Max was able to shed his navy sweater vest before his round even began. He started off with two pars, two birdies, and another par. Max was rolling along according to plan. Mitch, as his caddy, behaved himself by minimizing any praise, critique, or amusing remarks. It did not take much, however, to distract Max for just one critical moment. When he permitted his consciousness to settle briefly on the creek guarding the right side of the sixth fairway, and decided to make sure that he steered clear of the hazard, he failed to reorient himself onto a positive target line. His pull-hook stayed far from the creek—so far, in fact, that his drive bounced out of bounds on the left. Max went through his coping routine of releasing his frustration via a quick, inaudible curse, regrouping by taking a deep breath, and refocusing on his pre-shot routine for his second tee shot. His perfect drive was not enough, however. Still shaken by his two-shot penalty, his limbic system in fight-or-flight mode, Max hit his approach shot to the right of the green. He exploded from the bunker to within twenty feet but failed to read the tricky terrain of the green. His eyes could not believe Mitch's counsel that all putts at Birdies' Brook break toward the main road adjacent to the course. The resulting three-putt left him with a "snowman"—a big, fat, quadruple-bogey eight to record on his score card.

Max scrambled for a one-putt par save on number seven. Then he pulled his game back together for the next three holes, parring each comfortably. The eleventh hole was a 538-yard, uphill par-5 with a double dogleg. It was rated the second most difficult hole on the course. Trees lined the left and right and protruded at the first turn. A fairway bunker rested on the left at that curve, and another bunker lay in the middle of the fairway at the second dogleg. A pond extended into play in the right front of the green; the left was guarded by a pot bunker. Player and caddie concurred that it was a diabolically designed hole. Max teed up on the left side of the tee markers and visualized a draw down the left center. As planned, he shaped his shot to coincide with the first dogleg, landing it just right of the bunker. He was then tempted to sock a three-wood toward the narrow slot leading onto the green but thought it better not to gamble. Mitch nodded his agreement when Max requested his four-iron. It was perfect. So were his pitch to the green and the resulting five-foot putt. That birdie, and the ones on the short, par-4 thirteenth and par-3 fourteenth, put Max back to one under par for his round. He felt that he had a chance to shoot a score good enough to qualify for the Open.

That evaluation, as he stood on the fifteenth tee, was just enough to knock Max out of his "zone." Thinking prematurely of his potential success and no longer fully focused on the steps needed to hit the tee shot at hand, he pushed it into the trees on the right. Stymied behind one of them, he had to punch a five-iron onto the fairway and then hit a long iron to the green. His effort went left; he had pulled it. Alas, double bogeys do not get you into the U.S. Open Golf Championship. His three finishing pars left him one-over for the round, two shots behind the last qualifier.

It was a long, quiet drive back to Ebbinflo with the usually loquacious Mitch.

JD's experience with religion as a child had been compulsory and unenjoyable. His parents forced him to attend church services every Sunday, followed by Sunday school lessons, for several years. Between his consistent resistance, manifested by dawdling and tardiness more weeks than not, and his father's own less-than-fervent desire to attend, he was able to weasel his way out of going to church completely by the age of eleven. JD just could not see the point of organized prayer meetings. He felt that he had better things to do with his time.

Still, when the leaders and members of Holy Help scapegoated clergymen as largely responsible for perpetuation of the societal hassles that plagued him, JD felt some degree of conflict about the matter. Sure, Reverend Monotoning had been boring, but he had always seemed like an okay guy. He, and others like him, appeared rather harmless, too, and undeserving of violence against them. It took some rousing speeches by the charismatic Claude, and the powerful groundswell of group pressure, to persuade JD that clergymen not only had little value, as he had once believed, but could actually be damnable sources of suffering by the citizens of our nation.

JD recited the oath of allegiance to HH and agreed to maintain its vow of secrecy against all costs. He doubted that the future of the universe was at stake, as Claude had insisted, but who was he to take a chance? JD appreciated the caring friendships he was forming in the organization; it was like having a bunch of Dr. Treasures doting upon him, but without the need to see them by appointment only and to pay them for their ministrations. He did not mind the small-scale tithing that was required. And he felt vicariously proud to see the stout friend, Billy, of his friend, Mike, inducted into HH's Inner Circle—apparently to replace some guy named Frank. Maybe, just maybe, the religious leaders of our country were in cahoots with the politicians and corporate bosses who worked to keep oppressed guys like himself in their place.

That Sunday morning, Mitch felt apathetic, though not surprised, that he was on his way to pick up Priscilla to attend the wedding of one of her friends. After all, June is the marriage season. Most wedding ceremonies were relatively long and mundane, and the receptions tended to get "old" too fast; small talk can only stretch so far. It was an important event for Priscilla, of course, because of her friendship with the bride. Sometimes a wedding could turn out to be fun. Marriages are upbeat affairs, at least celebratory in spirit, and offered the opportunity to engage in intelligent conversations with some of the adults in a lighthearted atmosphere—in contrast with his interactions with troubled clients in his office. He wasn't too keen on the need to dress up for the occasion, preferring as strongly as he did for casual, tie-less attire. And dancing was not his cup of tea. So, all things considered, he felt prepared to endure, if not enjoy, the day.

"Holy high fashion, you look great," Mitch complimented Priscilla at her door.

"Thanks, handsome. And you should wear nice threads more often, yourself. Oh, I see an idea for a Christmas present for you—a couple of new ties to replace that one might be nice."

Mitch drove them toward the church in his sporty, silver, Japanese-built, two-door convertible, stopping for a quick car wash at Priscilla's insistence. At the church, as expected, Priscilla seemed to know everyone and Mitch nearly no one. By way of introductions while making their way to their seats, Mitch felt that he was warming up his smile muscles for the main event, the reception.

During the wedding ceremony, Mitch anticipated Priscilla's response and managed to refrain from poking a little fun at the appearance of some of the guests in the audience. He also restrained himself from engaging in some of the antics that he used to employ when bored in church as a child—doing a few 360-degree turns in his seat, dropping items onto the floor and then retrieving them, and humming tasteless ditties came to mind—but he could not help but daydream. When he glanced at Priscilla, she was giving the proceedings her rapt attention. She recited the prayers and sang the hymns with enthusiasm. She nodded in sync with the rhythms of the service and dabbed at her moist eyes with her handkerchief at various times. As the newly hitched couple strolled up the aisle, Priscilla beamed at them with a look of genuine rapture on her countenance. Mitch smiled politely and thought hopefully about the food awaiting them at the reception; maybe they would serve some of those hot little wieners that were toxic for the system but irresistibly tasty nonetheless.

The reception took place at the Deansville Rod and Gun Club. It was a nice facility, both indoors and out, but Mitch couldn't help but make a few choice quips about the assortment of heads of local game (mainly deer, bears, and beavers) and fish (muskellunge and Northern pike) that adorned the interior walls. Priscilla responded with looks to kill.

"If that woodchuck and muskrat were to elope, would they make little muskchucks or woodrats?"

"Your head might look good up there, Mitch. Glass eyes would become you."

Priscilla's own observations, on the other hand, were more focused on the event and its emotional impact on her. "What a lovely wedding ceremony it was. It was touching. This is so romantic, isn't it?"

Dabbing a hunk of dark bread into the spinach and artichoke dip, Mitch replied, "Yes, Garth and Bertha looked pretty hooked on one another. I hope that it works out for them."

"Why shouldn't it?" Priscilla inquired with a scowl.

"I've noticed that Garth has looked up and down every woman in the place while Bertha has danced with every man but him since the first tune. But that doesn't mean that they aren't madly in love and destined to stay together forever."

"And, my darling Mitch," Priscilla went on, with more than a little edge to her voice, "what do you think of marriage?"

Uh oh, he thought, *I've been expecting this topic of conversation for months now.* "It's good stuff."

"Good stuff? The sacred, blissful, enviable institution of wedlock is 'good stuff?' That's what you have to say about it, Dr. Treasure? You can be a real itch, Mitch."

Resisting quick temptation to express two more such rhyming words, those beginning with *b* and *w*, Mitch remained silent long enough to be spared from having to protect himself against the rising storm. The groom arrived to ask Priscilla to dance, and away she was whisked, with a reconstituted smile on her face.

Max enjoyed playing alone. He always had. Countless days, and joyous hours, of his childhood were spent playing golf by himself. Not only did he like playing alone, but he felt that his golfing skills had best been honed during solitary play and practice wherein he was free of social distractions. He could hit extra practice shots if he so chose. Without having to make conversation, search for others' wayward golf shots, await his turn to hit, and attend to the scores of playing partners, he could focus more fully on the sight and feel of any shot that lay before him. Furthermore, his zeal for the game was enhanced by the fantasy competitions that Max had conjured from an early age; by the time he was twenty, Max had imagined himself winning every major golf tournament at least five times, beating the likes of Jones, Sarazen, Hogan, Nicklaus, and Woods. If only he could play so well in reality.

Maybe his lapses in tournament golf were partly attributable to his penchant for solitary play at the expense of public competition. Perhaps he wasn't sufficiently accustomed to playing under pressure and scrutiny, learning to shield out distractions as they arose. He wasn't "tournament tough." Or maybe, Max sadly pondered, he just wasn't a very good golfer. Even though he could hit some fine shots on occasion, perhaps his inconsistency showed that he would never be able to pull it together sufficiently to make the grade in big-time competition.

Max took up aikido training because of his keen interest in Buddhist and Taoist philosophy—even though aikido does not teach any Zen or apply the principle of yin and yang explicitly—and long-time desire to train a martial art. It was always in the back of his mind, though, that it could help his golf. Mind-body coordination, calmness in action, centeredness, fluid motion, emphasis on mindfulness in the here and now—he could swear that aikido and golf are cousins. But drat! His improvements in golf had been painfully minute, if they existed at all, and he was still lucky if he could string together a few good holes, let alone two strong rounds. If he ever needed to use aikido to defend himself from attack by a gang of some sort, Max wondered if he would throw the first guy masterfully then get pummeled by the rest of the bunch. That would be par for the course for him.

Those were his thoughts as Max made his way around the back nine of Rolling Greens the Tuesday evening after his failure to get past the first round of qualifying for the U.S. Open. With self-doubt instead of positive imagery guiding his shots, and suffering from paralysis by analysis, he limped in with a round of four-over-par forty, his worst of the season. It was true what Mitch said about the power of self-fulfilling prophecies. Woeful was he.

Mitch still had snippets of the weekend wedding of Garth and Bertha in mind as he prepared himself to greet the unhappily married couple, Barry and Beth. Having clarified some of their expectations of one another at their first session, Mitch felt guarded optimism that they might compromise their differences and prioritize their relationship, warts and all. Wrong.

Beth and Barry entered his office and chose seats facing away from one another. He looked worried. She appeared tense and standoffish. It then came as no surprise that they had begun a trial separation; Beth had taken the children with her to live with her parents for the time being. Barry had time scheduled with the kids, who, understandably, were behaving in a more oppositional, emotionally labile manner. Mitch thought to himself about the statistics: Women who have negative perceptions of their mates are more likely than their counterparts to hold grudges, decline forgiveness, misjudge change, mistrust their husbands, and initiate separations.

A unified session began to verge on argumentation, so Mitch decided to "divide and conquer" by seeing Barry, and then Beth, individually for twenty minutes apiece. Barry felt dismayed and helpless. He had agreed to the fairness of the aforementioned expectations and had made what he thought were meaningful concessions and contributions at home. It appeared, however, that bridges had already caught fire. Mitch encouraged Barry not to give up but to prepare himself should the separation proceed to a complete marital split. Mitch did not take sides; his focus was on the well-being of each individual, and the welfare of their offspring, whether they stayed together or divorced. Beth spoke reasonably about the marriage, lamenting that it had gone south and wavering only slightly in her determination to steer clear of Barry unless there was evident improvement of their interactions. She believed, perhaps rightly, that the marital tension in the home was worse for the kids than their clinging reluctantly to a nuclear family. When reunited in the room, Barry and Beth seemed only slightly more at ease. Agreeing to disagree about certain issues yet together in their commitment to cooperate on behalf of the children, they told Mitch they'd get in touch to schedule another session.

Sitting in his second-story office and writing progress notes about the sad state of affairs between Barry and Beth, Mitch heard some sort of noise downstairs. He expected no one. He knew that the occupants of the first-floor offices had gone home for the day. There was another sound. Somebody had entered the building but had not ascended the stairs to his waiting area. He opened his door, leaned out, and called, "Hello. Who's there?" There was no answer. Neither was there any additional sound—for a few moments anyway. Then Mitch heard a clang of metal emanate from the vicinity of the downstairs bathroom. Mitch was not prone to paranoia—in fact, he worked hard to discourage anyone from living his/her life in fear—but caution was often worthwhile. He retreated into his office and picked up the *jo*, a short fighting staff, that he kept there for practicing his *katas* in his spare time. It also managed to give him a sense of security at times like these. Mitch called again from the landing of the stairs, "Hello. May I help you?"

Again, at first, there was no response. Then a timid male voice ventured, "Uh, hi. I'm, uh, I'm here to see the d-d-doctor."

"I'm Dr. Treasure." Mitch, mildly reassured by the meek voice, held the *jo* by his side, no longer in position to strike.

"Y-yeah, I'm here to see y-you." A slender, fair-haired young man slid shyly into view along the wall leading out of the bathroom toward the stairs.

"I usually see clients by appointment," said Mitch, without reprimand.

"I, I tried to call. But . . . I d-d-didn't." He was wringing his hands nervously.

"What's your name?"

"Uh, Henry. Henry Ziety. Most f-folks call me Hank." This information was delivered with only the briefest instant of eye contact with Mitch.

"I'll be down in a second." Setting the *jo* just inside his office door, Mitch grabbed his appointment book and descended the stairs. Hank's tension and gestures visibly intensified. "I'm glad that you're here, Hank," Mitch said in a soothing manner. "It's the end of my day, though, and I have to be somewhere soon. So, let's set up a time to get together. Can you come back tomorrow?"

"A-a-anytime," he stammered. "I don't have a j-job or a-a-anything."

Mitch scheduled a time to see Hank the following day. Giving him an appointment card and a wink of reassurance, Mitch urged reluctant Hank toward and out the front door.

He was curious to know what Hank had been up to before finally announcing his presence. Mitch walked into the bathroom. He'd have thought the sturdy old metal wastebasket, probably made half a century earlier, was destined to adorn the john for another fifty years. But it was crushed. The paper towel dispenser was dented on both sides. The broom that normally leaned against the corner instead lay on the floor, snapped in half. Hank was evidently stronger, and even more deranged, than he had appeared on first impression.

XI

LIAISONS

THE WEEKEND BEFORE THE U.S. OPEN GOLF CHAMPIONSHIP, in honor of it and its importance to the sport of golf, the Club Professional Association of Central and Western New York hosted an annual golf clinic. This year's event was conveniently located near Ebbinflo, at the next golf course west along Route 20A, the Tees 'N Trees Golf Club. Dr. Mitch Treasure, distinguished associate professor of psychology and coach of the golf team at Confluence College, was the invited keynote presenter. Not unexpectedly, he roped Max into helping him.

"Sure, you would rather be preparing to play golf with the big boys at Pebble Beach," Mitch had acknowledged, "but as a dyed-in-the-wool teaching professional, you'll be in your element at the clinic."

Max wasn't sure that he liked the label, even in light of his present level of discouragement as a tournament golfer, but he had to agree that he would find some enjoyment interacting with his fellow pros and helping to instruct some of the top young amateurs in the region.

It was a sunny Saturday morning at Tees 'N Trees. It was one of those mid-June days on which Max could not resist rebelling against the standard dress code of the PGA. Sure, he wore a regular-looking golf shirt, pale blue with the dark green Rolling Greens logo on the left chest portion. But it was a day to wear shorts, not full-length pants. He chose his loose-fitting denims. Only one other pro—his friend, Chick, from Blueberry Ridge—broke ranks along with him by daring to wear Bermuda shorts. Max could neither understand nor fully accept why professional golfers, and some country club players, were restricted in the range of apparel they could choose and were not routinely permitted to wear good-looking casual attire. He risked ticks and needed sunscreen while wearing shorts, but the departure from the dress code, with access to cool breezes, was worth it. Mitch, who might play in the nude if he could get away with it, looked less than professorial but fully comfortable in his tan cargo shorts and gold golf shirt.

About thirty club pros from the Niagara Frontier joined a dozen collegiate golf coaches and their teams for the Friday morning clinic. This course had been selected because of its ample practice facilities: a wide driving range with eight target greens, a chipping green with a practice bunker beside it, and two large putting greens. The group sat comfortably in the lush grass behind the practice tee as Mitch opened up proceedings, made appropriate introductory remarks, and then dug into the meat of his presentation with the periodic aid of a portable whiteboard.

"We're here to learn means of performance enhancement using sport psychology. Our goal is to develop in ourselves, and learn to teach others, optimal thinking patterns. Let's first examine appropriate mental attitude.

"In golf, as in all sports for that matter, we strive for quiet confidence balanced by a healthy dose of humility. Too much egotism that spills over into cockiness and arrogance is ultimately self-defeating due to distraction, away from task-related thinking, and anxiety, from fear of losing the competition and losing face with both oneself and others. Arrogance breeds contempt in others and alienation from peers; few people like a challenging, condescending, critical peer who puts them down and lords his or her sense of superiority over them. Reactions to one-upmanship and an "in your face" mentality range from shunning and avoidance, to vindictive desire to vanquish the egomaniac. The ideal is an even keel. Be outwardly gracious and self-effacing to foes and members of the media, but inwardly retain a strong resolve to do your best."

"Are you calling us 'cocky?'" asked Sam Sneadeker, the pro at Bent Grass. The golfers laughed, knowing from Mitch's good-natured style that he was anything but accusatory and detecting the mirth in Sam's voice.

"Au contraire, Monsieur," replied Mitch. "You wouldn't be here to learn if you were. I'm just spouting off about a problem that too often irks me in the world of sports, and trying to set you folks up for success. Competition is part of the fabric of society in general, and golf in particular. And winning is surely more enjoyable than losing. Confidence is good to have. However, we'll play our best golf with a cooperative attitude, one that incorporates the collective energies of partners, foes, and spectators alike. You may notice how certain top tour professionals refer to "we" to give credit for their play not just to themselves but also to their caddies, coaches, and other support staff. Furthermore, a win-win mentality is more constructive, less prone to the negative effects of emotional interference, than a win-lose mentality."

"So, Dr. Treasure, what is the best psychological formula for success?" inquired Ginger Grain, a pro from south of Buffalo.

"Thanks for the lead-in." Mitch winked. "During competition, as all of you golfers know, calm concentration works best. Let neither the small victories, such as birdies, nor setbacks, like bogeys, capture your emotions for more than a few seconds. Stay Zen, Gestalt, existential, and mindful. What I mean by that is focus on the here and now, intent on your imminent actions. We play best when we concentrate on the *process*, rather than the *outcome*, of athletic performance. Focus on the shot, not the score. Save any celebration or show of disappointment for the conclusion of the round. Vent on the nineteenth hole."

"Could you please be more specific? How do we maintain composure and focus on the present when we have present frustrations and future goals in mind?" queried Megan Hagen, another local colleague. Max always wondered whether or not she was related to the legendary pro, Walter.

"I'm heading there," continued Mitch. "First, though, I feel it is important to lay down some guiding principles. One is based on my belief that emotions are unavoidable. That is, emotional reactions to events happen automatically, too rapidly for you to be able to prevent them. However, as soon as you feel such an emotion, you *can* exert control through physical and cognitive intervention. For example, a bad golf shot is sure to stimulate a sense of frustration. But you need not slam your club into the turf in anger; instead, a sub-vocal curse, a deep breath, and a quick word to yourself, such as 'calm,' can dissipate your anguish fast enough to enable you to move on to your next shot with your composure intact."

"Easier said than done," Max blurted out. Many members of the audience nodded.

"Yes, sometimes it is," admitted Mitch. "It takes practice and self-discipline. We'll talk more about it later. Another important principle is based upon what I have learned in my aikido training, along with my buddy and your outspoken co-presenter, Max Azure. Incidentally, for the un-indoctrinated, aikido is a nonviolent art of self-defense. Because it evolved as a means of protecting oneself in potentially life-and-death situations and is designed to enable the weaker, slower, and smaller to overcome the stronger, faster, and bigger, its guiding principles seek to provide a mental edge—just like we strive for in golf. Aikido shows us that relaxation unifies the efforts of mind and body better than does muscular tension. When we approach any motor task with a calm demeanor, we are most likely to activate exactly the correct muscles, precisely the right amounts, to carry out the intended action to its utmost. For example . . . Max, please pick up your driver.

Max stood up and brought that club over near Mitch. "Grip it with all of your might," he instructed. "Tighten all of your muscles as you prepare to swing." Max addressed a teed-up practice ball with his body fully stiffened by muscular tension. Mitch wanted him to impart the same lesson to this group that he had demonstrated to Sister Rotini in her lesson a month before. "Have at it." Max could barely move, let alone take a lengthy backswing and hit through the shot. He was able merely to tap the ball off the tee. The audience chuckled. "As you can see," Mitch stated the obvious, "it's hard to swing a golf club with too many muscles over-activated. Activation of muscles irrelevant to the task at hand causes interference with smooth movement."

Mitch re-teed the ball and instructed, "Now relax, Max. Inhale deeply, then let out the air with a 'letting go' type of exhalation." Max sighed. "As you know, it feels much more natural, and works more effectively, to free up the golf swing. Starting from a feel of comfortable relaxation, you can trust that your hands will grip the club just tightly enough not to let it fly out of them, yet firmly enough to control the clubhead from your backswing through your downswing and follow-through. You can *trust* that just the right muscles needed to strike a golf ball, in your legs, back, arms, et cetera, will activate themselves at the right time and intensity to enable you to give it a ride."

Mitch nodded at Max. He swung and hit a drive that was straight but too high.

Derisive yet friendly oohs and ahs greeted his effort. "Okay, okay, so I skyed it. As Mitch said earlier, calm concentration, not practicing unreasonable tension while hitting, is most conducive to good golf."

"But that was one of your better drives, Max." Mitch could not resist the opportunity to prolong the humorous moment at Max's expense. Several mutual friends, and most noticeably his own golf team members, nodded and jokingly muttered their agreement.

"Now you are talking about and demonstrating physical aspects of golf, not the mental game," interjected Doug Divotski, assistant pro at Birdies' Brook.

"Yes, it looks that way," agreed Mitch. "But, you see, mind and body are one. Mental states and muscular activation blend into harmonious action."

"And tension kills tempo," added Sam. "We already know that golf is a game of calmness in action. So how do we achieve, maintain, and regain it? When we tighten up in competition, how can we loosen up quickly? Sometimes saying 'calm' and taking a breath don't cut it."

"This may sound like a cop-out, but you have to choose what works best for you, at that moment. Aikido offers the idea of keeping one-point—sending your awareness to a spot about two inches below your navel, and allowing your body weight to settle down toward that spot. By letting go of tension in the abdominal region, you become better centered and balanced. Some people find it effective to spend a few seconds relaxing their jaw muscles; by easing up this reservoir of tension, they find that their whole body relaxes. Try shrugging your shoulders tightly together and then letting them hang comfortably. Tighten, then release, or merely stretch any part of the body that feels uptight. You see," he concluded, nodding toward Doug, "in each case you willfully combine a mental with a physical intervention to ease your body and mind into a more relaxed state of preparedness for action."

Mitch went on to discuss the concepts of flow, zoning, and peak performance as they pertain to golf. He outlined steps for distraction control. He described how thoughts of past and future can flow smoothly through consciousness, enabling re-focus on the present. On the whiteboard, he sketched the relationship between anxiety and performance—an inverted "U" according to the Yerkes-Dodson Law—in order to show that there is a range of stress that helps, rather than hinders, performance. He solicited advice from the audience members regarding specific swing keys—words and images that make up effective pre-shot routines. He made the point that perfection is impossible; because the streams of consciousness and behavior, as in Nature, fluctuate biorhythmically, one cannot expect peak performance every instant of athletic activity. But the probability of excellent concentration, effort, and performance, Mitch explained, can be optimized by holistic training, coordination of mind and body, and mental rehearsal.

He concluded, "Don't neglect your overall wellness: nutritional foods, adequate rest, physical cross-training, emotional adjustment, social support, intellectual stimulation, and spiritual development. Each is a necessary, but not sufficient, ingredient of holistic health and golfing prowess.

Let's take a break now, then reconvene in fifteen minutes for the next portion of our clinic—where, Max?"

"Over by the large putting green, please," Max instructed.

"Trust is simultaneously a prerequisite to, and result of, solid putting," Max began after the recess. He felt pleased to be addressing his fellow pros, friends and foes alike, as well as the young collegiate golfers who would shape the not-too-distant future of their sport. "That is, self-confidence that you will strike the ball with proper force along the intended path increases the probability that this will indeed occur. Your reinforcement history and muscle memory combine to increase the odds that such prerequisite trust will be on call and available. For instance," Max said, actualizing his words as he prepared to hit a ten-foot putt, "here is the mental procedure through which I try to go for each and every putt. First, like most players, I look at the putt from the far side of the hole and the sides in order to read the terrain from all perspectives. Then I spend more time lining it up from behind the ball." He knelt there. "I visualize the path from the ball into the cup. I stay focused on that as I stand and approach my address position. Now standing perpendicular to the intended line, I do a quick mental run-through of aikido principles of keeping my one-point, relaxing, and settling down. I might also jiggle my shoulders and loosen my jaw, as Mitch suggested, to make sure that they are free of tension. During my two practice strokes, I again visualize the ball on a track rolling along the surface of the green and into the cup. As I address the ball itself, I again trace that path with my eyes, from ball to cup. Then I simply let it happen by stroking it thusly."

Whew! He made the putt. The crowd applauded and whooped it up, probably as much to celebrate the fact that Max had stopped talking as much as to cheer the fact that he had practiced what he preached. With a slight bow, Max asked, "Any questions?"

"You bet," responded his superior, the head pro at Rolling Greens, Stu Swingster. "What do you mean by 'reinforcement history,' and when the heck did you start using that weird putting grip?"

"I converted to this cross-handed grip, with my left hand lower down the putter shaft than my right, late last season. It helps me to keep both shoulders relaxed, especially the left one, all the way through the putt. I feel that I have a better pendulum action, for accuracy, and sense of touch, for distance. I read that Ben Hogan liked it, too, but just felt too embarrassed to employ it in tournament action. As for reinforcement history, I'll defer the question to the professional psychologist. Mitch?"

"The more success experiences you have—like the more putts you sink—the more confidence you will have in the style you employ to gain those rewards. Behavior predicts behavior. As Max said, such trust further enables you to relax and concentrate on the putt at hand, so you can continue to putt well."

"It's like a snowball effect," Max chimed in. "Success breeds success. Following an effective method routinely, with calm demeanor, improves the likelihood of good performance. And certainly, the same holds true for hitting full golf shots as well as for putting. For regular shots, I try to picture the flight path and landing spot of the ball; I imagine what it feels like for my body to make it happen, and then swing."

"It sounds too complicated," opined Ginger, "and time-consuming. Don't you suffer from 'paralysis by analysis?'"

"Alas, I do sometimes," Max confessed. His mind flashed back to the practice round through which he had recently suffered after his bruising self-defeat while trying to qualify for the Open. "My explanation today was a blow-by-blow account of my thought process. Usually, at least when I am playing well, I streamline the whole thing to 'see it, feel it, do it.'"

"That sounds better," affirmed Ginger.

"Bear in mind, though, that our thoughts move very rapidly," interjected Mitch. "Lots of words and pictures fly through our consciousness in the span of just a few seconds. In between golf shots, there is plenty of time for on-task, as well as distracting, thinking."

"So, my objective here has been to describe what I think and do to maximize coordination of mind and body in the golfing context," Max resumed, "and to give you an example. I have given you my outline of how to be absorbed in the present, not to get ahead of myself, therefore increasing my chances of playing 'in the zone.' Each of you may have your own personal ritual for approaching each golf shot in the interest of playing your best. You must tailor your style to suit yourself."

Max did not know if it was a case of learning by teaching, forcing himself to practice what he preached, or relaxing with good friends. But when he went out for a post-seminar round of golf that afternoon, he shot a bogey-free, four-under-par score of sixty-eight. He dared to hope that he was over his slump.

Was it social? Was it business? Why did Detective Southworth ask Max and Mitch to meet him at the tavern of their choice—O'Duffers' Pub in this case—that Saturday evening? Instead of the badly tailored jacket and mismatched tie in which they had seen him previously, the police officer wore casual slacks and golf shirt for the occasion. His biceps and belly protruded noticeably. Whatever he wanted, they appreciated his gesture of buying the first round of beers. He confirmed that he was off duty by ordering one for himself.

"I bet that you guys played golf in that beautiful weather we had today," detected the officer.

"You've got that right, Detective. Mitch and I taught a seminar together this morning, but we managed to squeeze in a round in the afternoon."

"If you don't mind, lay off the 'Detective' label for now and call me Bud. For one thing, I'm off duty. For another, I don't want to draw undue attention to our conversation."

"Right on, Bud. Do you play golf?" Max asked.

"I won this shirt in a tournament," he boasted with a smile. "I wasn't too keen on winning the award for taking the most putts in the annual Police Association outing, but it was a nice consolation prize."

"Maybe you should take a lesson from this guy," suggested Mitch, pointing his thumb at Max, "before the next tournament."

"Yeah, I just might do that. And I suppose that you, Doc, could offer me some psychological mumbo-jumbo to help me play better too."

"Of course I could!" enthused Mitch. "In your line of work, you probably need some stress management techniques. Golf is a game of relaxation, after all."

"Well, maybe you guys can give me some golfing advice and give me tips to reduce my stress here tonight. You see, there's a charity golf tournament coming up in a couple of weeks that I plan to play in. I would just as soon not make a fool of myself."

"It wouldn't, by any chance, be the tournament at my club, Rolling Greens, to honor the memory of Reverend Eagleton and raise money for his two favorite charities, the Wholly Holy Christian Academy and the Junior Golf Association of Central New York?"

"The very one. Good deduction, Mr. Azure."

"Are you playing for the love of golf or the protection of the tournament participants?" asked Mitch.

"Another astute assumption. My, my, you guys are good."

"And since we're approaching that subject," Max said, "may I ask how the investigation is going?"

"We have a few leads; I can say that much. But we have nothing solid. In fact, one of the reasons that I asked you fellows here tonight is to pick your brains about a few things—unofficially, of course, and off the record. I hope that you don't mind."

"Why unofficially? How come you didn't just ask us to come to your office for interviews? You know that we'd be glad to do anything to help," responded Mitch.

"Because I wanted the freedom to relax, free associate, and explore some ideas that may or may not make sense. I wanted you guys to feel similarly comfortable to take off on any tangent that might, inadvertently, help put this puzzle together. Besides, sometimes it's refreshing to mix business with pleasure." He took a sip of his pint of Scot's Suds. Max and Mitch glanced at each other, both probably thinking that they may have underestimated the wits of this public servant.

"What's on your mind?" Max inquired.

"We, meaning the collective law enforcement agencies, can't get a handle on how those Holy Help thugs, if that's who they are, pick their targets. I've said that I don't get out on the links much, but I doubt that I'll ever see a priest playing golf in a stiff white collar, a nun swinging a club in her habit, or a rabbi out there in his yarmulke and prayer shawl."

"No, me neither," Max concurred, "but if ever it'll happen, it could be in that tournament." They all chuckled at the image. "Perhaps the culprits scout their prey in the pro shops. Every golfer signs in before playing. We have lots of people filtering in and out of the pro shop in search of equipment. I'm usually too busy to pay much attention to who browses or buys. And the registration sheet is out on the front counter for all to see. The public is also welcome to mill around the clubhouse, dine or drink, practice putting, or hit range balls."

"And the yellow pages or the phone book, available online or in libraries, includes a listing of all local clergy," added the detective, "so maybe it's not such a difficult process of selection after all. And pros like you wouldn't notice strangers hanging around?"

"Often not."

"Hmmm. Another thing I've been wondering about is the organization itself. What makes it tick? Why would people join it? How do its leaders recruit members? Plenty of folks are unhappy about their lives, but they don't all join a murderous organization as a result. What are your ideas on that subject, Doc?"

Mitch and Max had previously discussed this, so they had some thoughts on the matter. "As you say, Detective, I mean Bud, a lot of people feel unhappy and frustrated," replied Mitch. "Many turn to religion for solace. Adding spiritual meaning to life helps us maintain perspective and aids our ability to cope with the inevitable ups and downs of experience. But this particular group, which I suspect would best be called a cult, must have a unique appeal. History teaches us that violent cults are often based in prejudice and paranoia."

"Paranoia? Isn't that some sort of fear? What does feeling scared have to do with it?" inquired Bud.

"People who fear others often decide to strike first, to attack the source of anxiety. You know, get them before they get you. Paranoia is, after all, an irrational fear. It's exaggerated way out of proportion to an actual threat. Adolf Hitler felt not only that Jews were a source of miserly misery to the German people, but also a danger to do more harm because of their business acumen. Hence, he wanted them removed from the country or, failing that, exterminated. He was able to sell his irrational scapegoating of the Jews to the German people by means of shared paranoia. His fiery rhetoric made his listeners afraid of whatever enemy he cared to name."

"Interesting theory, Doc."

"The other relevant, and fascinating, feature of paranoia is the self-righteousness that often accompanies it. Paranoia can breed delusions of grandeur. Some severely paranoid individuals feel so egotistical, so correct in their analysis that their cause is just and that their good must triumph over evil, that they feel compelled to lord their mastery over others. The stereotypical psychotic that insists that he is Jesus Christ is not merely a religious nut, but also someone who overcompensates for his paranoid fears by convincing himself that he is almighty. Hitler felt that he was a superior member of the German master race, destined to rule the world, and he persuaded many German people of their superior status. It is very seductive to hear that you are better than others."

"So, help me get this straight. You're saying that the leader of Holy Help may be some paranoid lunatic, some guy who feels superior to others, angry at those who have tried to keep him in his place or frustrated him in the past, and eager to wipe out his enemies."

"Yes, that's the gist of it."

Max jumped in. "And he recruits followers by delivering a message of outrage and hope—scapegoating the clergy for causing their pain and suffering, and promising them a wonderful future through violent means."

"And the cult leader delivers. Not only does he offer a new belief that explains a difficult life crisis, but he also gives immediate reward by reducing anxiety or depression in the receivers of his paranoid message," clarified Mitch. "Furthermore, much of this could be based in religion. Religion gives many benefits to society, but unfortunately it tends to be separatist at the same time. Some religions teach that their path is the most holy—better than others. Their practitioners might feel content to practice their faith in a self-satisfied manner, or choose to proselytize in the interest of 'saving' others, affirming the justness of their faith and growing in number and stature. More members bring more money and sense of power too. Other religions go farther. They seek to eliminate rivals in order to please God or themselves."

Max carried Mitch's thinking a step further. "It seems to me that numerous massacres have occurred, and wars fought, over religion than over most other issues. The Crusades, the Inquisition, various pogroms, and the Holocaust targeted Jews. Strife between Lebanese Christians and Muslims, between Irish Catholics and Northern Irish Protestants, and between Indian Hindus and Pakistani Muslims are just a few more examples. The Islamic concept of *jihad*, or holy war, seems to underlie modern-day conflicts worldwide. Holy Help appears to be kicking up its own little holy war, on a small but evil scale."

"People are drawn to religious beliefs," Mitch concluded. "They can be compelling and persuasive to potential cult members. Once they are hooked into the warped belief system that offers relief from their woes, unfortunately, they often accept superfluous aspects of the cult. Individuals grow increasingly dependent on fellow cult members for emotional support, psychologically distance themselves from sane members of society, and grow more willing to act out against civilization."

"Gee, you fellas have given this matter more thought than I expect-ed," commented the detective. "If I buy you another beer, I wonder what else you'll have to say."

It seemed like a throwback to old times when Max took Melody out for a date to play miniature golf. It was just the right speed for both of them. Being athletic and feeling fond of him, she was tempted to take up the game of golf, but she felt intimidated by his relative expertise at the sport. For his part, maybe Max did not feel ready to test his patience in teaching this special beginner, one for whom he cared so much. The miniature golf course, with its slick putting surfaces, mechanical obstacles, and multiple tubular pathways toward and away from targets, leveled the playing field for them. It was relaxing and fun.

So was the rest of the evening. With neither of them having any pressing early morning appointments lined up for Monday, Melody was in no hurry to leave Max's apartment, and he felt no inkling to take her home. It was time once again to explore the wonderful world of massage.

"Max, what are you doing?" she tittered as she wiggled away to avoid the ticklish feeling of his fingers creeping down her spine.

"Ah, this is the controversial cranio-scapular exploratory technique. I learned it once in a *Jin Shin Do* class."

"Well, it tickles, and you can just send it right back where you got it."

"Oh, yes, that's because I forgot something." He grabbed a stick of cocoa butter and began lubricating his fingers with it.

"That smells nice, at least," Melody responded. "Chocolatey."

"Would you like to taste some while I massage you?"

She rolled halfway off her back, on the living room rug, to see the stick. "You want to feed me cocoa butter? Byech!"

"No, silly, but this might melt nicely in your mouth." Max reached into the drawer of the end table and pulled out a bar of Swiss dark chocolate.

"Oh, you shouldn't have," she cooed. "You know I can't resist that stuff."

"Yes, the better to play with your scapulas, my dear," he retorted in his best imitation of Bela Lugosi, a.k.a. Count Dracula.

Melody settled back onto the Oriental rug with a small piece of chocolate on her tongue and began to relax visibly as Max knelt behind the top of her head and engaged alternately in three different massage movements: pushing down on her trapezius muscles with his thumbs, allowing them to glide gradually from neck to shoulders; grabbing those same trapezius muscles and pulling them gently toward himself; and reaching his hands, palms up, as far down her back as he could without her having to move, then extending his fingers upward and sliding them along either side of her spine toward himself. He finished that movement by lifting her head, keeping his fingers pushing gently into the muscles to a point up to the base of her cranium, thereby applying soothing traction, before gingerly setting her head back down onto the floor. Several iterations of this sequence made Melody look as though she had drifted into slumber. But she was well aware when Max paused.

"Max, that is *so* relaxing." She stirred, stretched, and started to rise. "May I try it on you?"

"Sure. First, let me put on some music to massage by."

He went over to his stereo cabinet and uncovered the turntable. Then he proceeded across the room to the cabinet that stood by the bookcase containing some of his golf trophies.

Melody asked, "Are those actually stacks of wax under your plaques, Max?"

"Musical reproductions come in all forms, my dear," said his faulty imitation of W. C. Fields. "I'm looking for some old-fashioned mood music, the better to enchant you."

When Spike Jones and his Wacky Wakakians launched into their rousing and comical "Hawaiian War Chant," Melody's laughter took her relaxation to a new level.

"You are a nut," she commented. "That's music to massage by?"

"Well, perhaps I could do better." At song's end, he keyed up a selection of mellow instrumental tunes on his MP3 player and requested, "May I please receive my massage on the bed in my sleeping chamber?"

"Oh, naughty thinking, Max. I like it."

The chocolate and cocoa butter accompanied them into the bedroom, and Melody's massaging hands began to wander, both soothingly and excitingly, over expanding areas of Max's flesh. "This is what I like in a relationship—hands-on experiences," he quipped. His hands began to reciprocate her manipulations until, one by one, their articles of clothing were shed and cast aside.

"You feel so strong, Max, and delightful to touch."

"You're pretty firm yet smooth, yourself. Exercise makes us sexy, eh?"

"And lubricious, sweetcakes," she reported as she kissed him deeply.

Soon, but not too soon, amidst caresses and chuckles, romantic mutterings led to sexual gymnastics. Max and Melody managed somehow to harmonize smiles and humor with passion. It took a while for their giggles to subside and their breathing to return to normal.

Their subsequent cuddle was interrupted by a call from nature. Max stirred and announced, "I'd like to skip to the loo, my darling."

"May I please be privy to what you plan to do in there?"

"Phase I entails the process of eliminating some of the by-products of metabolism."

"And Phase II?"

"I'm a lean, mean, but unclean machine. I thought that I would do both of us a service by taking a shower."

"And would you like to have some company—for Phase II, I mean?"

"Let's go with the flow."

It took a bit of persuasion, but Mitch managed to get JD out to the golf course for a nine-hole round with Max that Tuesday evening. It seemed that JD had a conflicting engagement, as well as reluctance to try his hand at a game that evoked some strong memories and conflicting emotions, but Mitch convinced him that this was the next step in his therapy. As for Max, he had planned to catch up on some bookkeeping in the office. He also hesitated to meddle in one of Mitch's therapeutic relationships, even though he had promised to uphold the same standard of confidentiality to which Mitch subscribed. In the end, despite resistance in both parties, golf won out.

"Max, I'd like you to meet JD Smith. JD, this is Mr. Maxwell Azure, golfer extraordinaire." They shook hands.

"Nice to meet you, JD, and welcome to Rolling Greens."

"Thanks, Mr. Azure."

"I understand that you need to borrow some clubs. Dr. Treasure told me that you used to play, and enjoy, the game, but that you have not been on a golf course in years."

"I used to play with my dad when I was a kid. Now I probably have no idea how to swing a club."

Max walked into the club storage room behind the pro shop and emerged with an old golf bag filled with late-model clubs. "I think that you'll like these, JD. They are a set of last year's clubs that we lent out for people to take onto the range or course—you know, to try them out and decide whether or not to buy a set of them. They're still in good shape."

JD examined the clubs and his face lit up. "These are pretty cool. Thanks!"

"And here are some balls and tees; I find extras every round," offered Mitch. "As for a glove, let's see what Mr. Azure has in stock."

Max fitted a glove to JD, purchased—at wholesale price—as a gift from Mitch to JD. As his gift to his friend and the young man, Max waived the greens fee.

JD was nervous as a cat on the first hole. With his shoulder muscles nearly in knots, he topped his first few shots. But as they walked and talked their way down the next few fairways, he gradually relaxed. While he couldn't keep up with Max and Mitch in terms of distance and accuracy, he began to display a smooth, natural swing.

"Are you sure you haven't played for years?" Max asked, eliciting a blush of pride from JD. "You're looking pretty good out here."

"Even my parents don't know this, but I sometimes watch golf tournaments on TV. It can be a little boring to watch, but something about it gets my attention."

"Well," responded Mitch, "I'd say that you've watched some of that golf rather closely. Either your observational learning is solid, or you managed to hold onto your swing from when you were a kid, or both."

"Anyway, you've got game," Max summarized.

JD responded by topping his next drive. The trio laughed good-naturedly. Max was pleased and impressed to see that the seventeen-year-old displayed none of the acts of frustration—pounding a club into the turf, throwing a ball or club, cursing, sulking—typical of many young players, himself included. This lad seemed better than "normal"; Max felt curious to know what unobservable problems warranted his counseling with Mitch.

When they reached the tee of the 178-yard, par-3 eighth hole, JD asked, "What club do you guys usually hit here?"

"It's a five- or six-iron for me, depending on the wind," replied Mitch.

"I like to hit a seven, but as Dr. T said, the wind might shift me to a six-iron," Max stated.

"Today, with the wind coming from left to right, and slightly into our faces, and the pin on the right, with the mild temperature, I bet that a seven-iron is the club for you, Mr. Azure."

"That's quite the thorough analysis, JD," Max responded with his eyebrows raised and lips pursed. "But with that breeze angling toward us, don't you think a six-iron is called for?"

"Not the way you're swinging, and with the ball carrying farther in the warm air."

"Okay, let's go straight for the center of the green with the seven and see if that breeze nudges it toward the pin." Max sculpted the shot just as he had described it. It landed on the front right portion of the green, checked up, and rolled lazily to within six feet of the cup.

"Thanks, JD. That was a good call. By the way, I've been wondering," Max confessed, "What is your actual name? What do the initials JD stand for?"

"That's it. That's all there is. That's the name my parents gave me."

Mitch piped in. "That's what you told me previously. But as I said at the time, I find that hard to believe."

"Well, maybe JD stands for something. But it's what I've always been called. Besides, you guys would make fun of me."

"Aha, so JD *is* a set of initials," added Mitch in a bemused but not sarcastic manner.

"We're just curious. We won't laugh at your name or tell anyone, JD," Max encouraged.

"Jah Duh," JD mumbled in unintelligible fashion.

Mitch and Max fixed him with puzzled stares and hit him with a simultaneous, "What?"

"John Doe. John Doe Smith is my name. There, I've said it. Pretty funny, huh?"

"That is an unusual name, but I find nothing very amusing about it," Max reacted.

"Unusual? Why, it must be the most common name there is," added JD.

"JD, that's only a stereotype. It's a cultural myth," Mitch opined. "Sure, there may be lots of 'John Smiths' around, but I bet you'd be hard pressed to find any 'John Does' in the telephone book."

"And surely few people, if any, have that entire name. John Doe Smith—that's a unique name. And JD? That's a cool nickname," Max said sincerely.

"Gee-whiz, you guys are something else. Either you're darn good at kissing up to me, or you really think that my name is okay."

"Hey, it's just your given name, not even the one you use. We like *you*, regardless of your name," enthused therapeutic Mitch, "and we plan to keep calling you nothing other than 'JD' unless you want us to change."

JD smiled. Then his eyes narrowed in thought and he took their conversation in its logical direction. "So, Dr. Treasure. It's Mitchell, right?" Mitch nodded. "And Mr. Azure—you're Maxwell, eh?" Max nodded. "What are your middle names?"

"Oh, well, is that polite, Mitch, for a young adult to ask such personal information of his elders?" Max evaded.

Mitch danced with him. "No way, José—and José is not Max's middle name, JD. No, I don't think that it's his place to pry into our business like that."

JD, too tickled to concentrate, hit his twenty-foot putt thirty feet. "C'mon, let's have 'em, elders. But do I have to promise not to laugh?"

They told him. He not only laughed. He took three more putts on that green and teased them all the way down the ninth hole.

XII

CRAZY ABOUT THIS & THAT

MAX'S GOLF STUDENTS WERE HAVING MIXED SUCCESS applying what they had learned in his lessons with them. Sister Rotini, hoping to make a good showing in the charity tournament that coming Saturday, saw him for a tune-up on Wednesday afternoon. She was swinging well, fully turning on her backswing, pausing briefly, nicely shifting her weight, and extending herself into a complete follow-through. She could do this because, following Max's advice, she had relaxed her grip and slowed down her tempo. No longer merely trying to hit the ball, with a short and tense stab at it, she was swinging the golf club and letting it strike the ball in its path.

"You know, my spiritual upbringing has taught me to accept the bad with the good, to understand that God fills our lives with pains as well as pleasures. But, by all that is holy, I swear that golf is more fun when I play it well!" They both smiled heartily at her honest appraisal.

As for Larry Bogart, with whom Max worked next that afternoon, his progress was more uneven.

"Max, that putting lesson you gave me has done a world of good. I'm scoring fewer snakes and more mongooses. However, I still can't get past bogey golf. With my short game now humming, my driving has gone to pot. I'm spraying my tee shots all over the course. I need the one-putts just to save bogeys."

"That's golf for you, Bogey. It's hard to put the entire game together. It makes you marvel at how the touring pros manage it, doesn't it?"

"Yes, I guess so. But Max, give me some help here. Tell me why my long game went south when my short game improved. And tell me how to fix the problem!" His frustration was palpable. Bogey took his golf seriously. In response to his anguish, Max momentarily felt tempted to refer him to Mitch for some direct therapeutic assistance. Bogey needed to gain self-acceptance of his limitations, not just lower golf scores. For now, Max contented himself to play amateur psychologist and professional golf instructor.

"Bogey, I meant what I just said about the pros. It is truly challenging to put together an all-around excellent golf game. As one aspect of your game improves, another part often worsens. As a result, the best mindset for golf, among pros and amateurs alike, is one that expects great play but readily accepts each setback. We want to cope well with golfing adversity. Keep the faith. Do you know what I mean?"

"Yeah, I get you. But to hell with faith. I'm just looking for improvement, not miracles."

"Right. The more upset and uptight you get about your shortcomings, however, the worse you'll play. Now, about your driving—let's set up a balanced schedule of practice shots of all ranges, long and short. Tee up a ball."

Max had him hit some drives. Indeed, he hit them every which way but straight. His head moved too freely, he was releasing his grip and flopping his wrists at the top of his backswing, and his follow-throughs often pulled him off-balance toward his toes.

"See what I mean?" he asked, with the weight of the world seemingly on his shoulders.

Max had Bogey lay down his driver in order to do some brief breathing and centering exercises. Still clubless, Max directed him to swing with his arms only. He settled into a pattern of balanced movement. With his driver in his hands again, he swung eight or ten times in a free and easy manner. Max confirmed that relaxation is important but that a golf grip needs to be firm enough to control the club. When Max slipped a ball onto a tee before him and asked him to swing as he had been doing, Bogey connected well but sliced it. "Now, take aim at that flag at the two-hundred-yard mark." He hit a beauty.

"Thanks, Max. I think I get your point. Sometimes I have to back off, regroup, relax, and get back on track."

"And not demand too much of yourself."

"Exactly."

And speaking of demanding a lot, Roger Dodge arrived promptly for his second lesson on Thursday after school. For his own personal safety and the protection of life and property around them, Max was tempted to arm him with plastic practice balls instead of real range balls. However, he took a deep breath and prepared to take the bull by the horns.

"Howdy, Roger. Are you ready for our lesson?"

"Yeah, I wanna hit a lot of balls today."

"I bet you do," Max replied, forcing his face to relax into a smile, "but we're going to take our time hitting today. I'll tell you why."

Max explained that Roger was there to learn to improve. They could only do that one step at a time. Roger shifted about uneasily, only half-listening to his coach's message. Then Max grabbed his attention.

"Watch this. Haste makes waste." Max rushed up to a ball on the lesson tee with his seven-iron in hand, hurriedly swung at it, and sent it scuttling along the ground to the left as he lost his balance. Roger laughed. "Haste makes waste," he repeated, again swinging wildly and whiffing this time. Roger laughed more. Max swung once more, this time at a measured pace. The ball exploded off the turf, soaring high, straight, and far. "Slower is better." Roger nodded receptively. "Golf is a great game, Roger, and the better you learn to play it, the better you'll like it."

Children will be children, so Roger did not fully spare Max his hijinks that day. But he was surely more attuned to what Max said and demonstrated during the balance of their lesson.

Wayne Windham rounded out Max's day on the lesson tee. The usually good-natured oaf powerfully sprayed shots hither and yon but, uncharacteristically, showed flashes of temper. He cursed under his breath after mishitting two shots in a row.

"This frustrating game can make us feel a little edgy, can't it, Wayne?"

"No, it's just a recreation, a game." He denied his visible anger.

As he had done with Larry Bogart, Max had Wayne step aside from actually hitting balls to unwind a bit by swinging with his arms only. Unlike Bogey, however, Wayne appeared unable to let go of his tension and mood. He pounded a few subsequent shots into the fairway, but he alternated those with more off-target swings. The lesson was mutually unsatisfying.

Mitch encountered similar, though more serious, challenges during the course of his professional week. While Max was busy blending golf, grins, and spirituality with Sister Rotini, Mitch was trying to cope with teaching Henry Ziety to cope.

A couple of weeks back, Hank had arrived promptly for his second session but, wracked with nerves, had been too timid to knock on Mitch's door. When Mitch searched for him in the waiting room, he found Hank seated behind the door, looking small as he nibbled his fingernails. Their session had resulted in some improvement of Hank's ability to converse with minimal stammering. On this day, their third appointment, Hank had regressed to the point of having to work up his courage by squeezing various items in the downstairs bathroom again. Mitch investigated the telltale sounds emanating from there.

"Hank, is that you?" he called through the door. There was no response. "Sorry," replied Mitch as he turned to climb the stairs back to his office. He wondered if he would soon be dealing with a second bathroom marauder.

"Is, is that you, D-D-Dr. Treasure?"

"Yes, Hank." Mitch shook his head and smiled to himself. "It is I. Whenever you're ready to come out, feel free. I'm glad that you're here."

Mitch decided to wait the ninety seconds or so that it took before the door handle of the restroom slowly turned and Hank stuck out his head. "Hi, Doctor," he mumbled after a fleeting glance at Mitch.

The administrator of the agency that provided supported living services to Hank had told Mitch the week before, with Hank's consent, that the young man presented no threat to society. He tended to wander the streets too frequently but aroused no complaints as a result. He took part, with reluctance, in organized recreational opportunities afforded by the agency. His tendency to damage property appeared, in large part, to be confined to Mitch's toileting facility.

"So, Hank, I had a nice conversation with Val Paksil, the director of the agency that provides you with housing. She assured me that you are an okay guy."

Hank blushed without looking at Mitch.

"In fact, she told me that you act kind to others, seem well-coordinated in sports, and take good care of your belongings." Oops! When praise conflicts with one's negative self-image, a state of cognitive dissonance is created. Hank scrunched his body as he began to moan and rock gently in his chair. "But enough about that," Mitch tried to backtrack. "Hank, look at this." Mitch got up and walked to his table on which he had set up the Lowenfeld Mosaic Task. He beckoned Hank to join him, thus successfully breaking him out of his nervous funk.

Hank moved slowly, hesitantly into and through the process of creating a mosaic design with the tiles provided. But he eventually provided a more detailed and imaginative design than Mitch had expected. There appeared to be considerable intelligence harbored within Hank's shell of insecurity. Fueled by increasingly positive expectations for his client, Mitch moved their session into modeling and rehearsing prosocial skills, followed by some modest short- and long-term goal-setting. Hank's overall prognosis improved from dismal to workable in Mitch's estimation; in fact, there was even a chance that Hank could pull himself together sufficiently to become a contributing member of society. Mitch would, however, have to influence Hank to pursue the prerequisite skills to become a carpenter, mason, or other hands-on worker; his other ambition, to become a psychologist, might have to be deterred.

Besides planning to continue their sessions together, Mitch referred Hank to two outside sources of assistance. "Hank, I strongly encourage you to attend at least one meeting of Neurotics Anonymous. I think that you'll feel a certain kinship with the helpful members of that support group. I would also like you to undertake a vocational assessment at the Adult Education Center. You'll have fun experiencing a variety of tasks and tools." Hank's assent was lukewarm at best, but after he had departed for the day, Mitch telephoned Ms. Paksil with the details about these recommendations.

It was not yet time for Len's session, but Mitch thought that he detected a sound outside his office. He checked the waiting room, and sure enough, Len was pacing its confines in his focused, conscientious manner. "I know that I'm early, Doc, but do you mind if I come in? I'm pretty uptight today."

"No problem, Len, come on in."

Len hesitated. "Do you mind?" he inquired hopefully.

Catching his drift, Mitch retreated into his office and closed the door to await the customary series of fifteen knocks. Upon entry, Mr. Tourette embarked upon his ritual of pacing back and forth six times, but he added several pirouettes to his routine.

"I must say that your spin moves are looking good, Len, but I thought that we agreed for you to cut back, not expand, your behavioral repertoire."

"Well, yes, but I told you that I'm feeling pretty wired today, Doc." Len circled his chair twice, like a dog looking for a suitable napping or toileting place, before falling into it. He followed this with a brief explosion of exclamations: "Fudge! Clockstrucker! Great Caesar's Ghost! Lordy, lordy, holy roly-poly!"

Mitch spared Len any additional lecture. "What's going on, Len? Tell me what's on your mind today."

"Doc, do you remember that little lady I mentioned, the vixen that works down the hall from me?"

"Mm-hmm."

"She asked me out. At least, I think that's what she did." It amazed Mitch that Len could speak so quickly without tripping over his tongue. "This morning she told me that a friend of hers gave her two tickets to this Saturday's Buffalo Bisons' game, because the friend cannot go, so she asked me if I like baseball, and holy guacamole, what could I say?"

"I don't know. What *did* you say?"

"I couldn't say that I hate baseball. You know me, Doc; I can't sit still for anything. And baseball? The pitcher waits for the sign from the catcher, shakes his head, awaits another sign, nods in agreement, goes through some little thirty-second stretching thing, eyes the runner at first base, looks back to the plate, turns and throws to first, gets the ball back, and starts the process all over again. We're talking hours of sitting and spectating for the sake of a few dozen seconds of action. I like suspense as well as the next guy—well, no, I don't—and baseball makes me antsy as all get-out."

Mitch made no attempt to hide his amusement at this description of baseball. But he managed to ask seriously, "So, what did you tell her?"

"I *love* baseball. I've always loved the game. I'd be thrilled to be able to go to a game."

"And . . . ?"

"And she handed me the two tickets."

"So, was she asking you to go to the game with her, or merely to take the tickets off her hands?" Mitch inquired in response to this curve ball.

"I don't know. At that instant, her boss walked up and summoned her to his office. I haven't seen or heard from her since then. I was on the run, and the few times I looked for her, she wasn't there. What am I gonna do, Doc?" Len asked imploringly.

"I'm not sure. But now I understand why you've added those pir-ouettes to your pacing." While Len took the cue and started to walk about the floor, Mitch requested, "Please tell me her first name, Len, just for future reference."

"Amelia. I looked it up in a dictionary of names. It means 'busy' or 'energetic.'"

"Sounds like a good match, Len. I wish you luck."

Their therapy session ended with a three-pronged plan for Len either to speak with Amelia directly at his first opportunity on Friday, send her an e-mail query, or leave a note at her desk regarding the baseball game at hand.

After Len departed, it was time for Mitch to move into the romantic life of Haley. Ms. Sunnation, unlike Len, whose romance might not have been delusional in nature, had a psychedelic encounter with the subject of her affections.

"I saw my high school sweetheart today," she started when ensconced in Mitch's cozy office chair. "It had been years since I last saw Vince, but it was just like old times."

"Really," responded Mitch, masking his skepticism. "Where did you see him?"

"In my apartment." Haley resided in a supported living situation, a two-bedroom apartment that she shared with another young woman who, like Haley, required loose supervision of her affairs. "He was in my living room when I got up this morning. He was sitting there on the sofa, looking just as young and handsome as he did when I dated him ten years ago."

Mitch knew from her birthdate that Haley had been out of high school at least fifteen years, so her statement confirmed his suspicion that Vince's visit had been merely an imaginary one. "So, you were glad to see him today?"

"Oh yes, and judging by our interaction, I'd say he was happy to see me too."

"You two talked for a while?"

"Yes, about old times mainly. I sure hope that he drops by to see me again soon."

"Haley, you may not want to hear this old line from me again, but I have to say it: I find it hard to believe that Vince actually visited you today."

"Aw, go on. Of course he did. Surely you believe me this time."

"As in the past, I believe that you saw Vince in your apartment this morning. But it was only an image of him, not the actual guy in the flesh."

"Oh. Bummer. Darn. That would explain how he disappeared so quickly without even saying goodbye."

"Yes, it would," added Mitch agreeably. He worked hard to obscure the blend of sympathy and frustration that he felt at that moment. Poor Haley. It was a shame that there was nothing that he or anyone else could do to nudge her schizophrenic mind into a pattern of down-to-earth thinking.

And speaking of misperceptions, Mitch had the dubious distinction of beginning to wind down his week with a telephone conversation with the parents of Ned Kopresis. Mitch had grown to be guardedly optimistic about Ned. The latest report from the school psychologist, Binet Wechsler, noted improving grades, a few budding friendships, and nearly a month without a toileting accident in school. This day, Mitch was surprised when Ned failed to show up for his Friday afternoon appointment. With a sense of foreboding in the pit of his stomach, he telephoned Ned's home. Mrs. Kopresis did not hesitate to inform Mitch that the family would no longer be needing his services. They were now taking Ned to a psychiatrist, Dr. Script, who had started administering a variety of medications to help alleviate the problematic symptoms that troubled the parents about Ned.

Mitch could not help but ask if the doctor had prescribed any medications for her and Ned's father. "Why, no, of course not," responded the self-assuredly deluded Mrs. Kopresis. "His father and I are doing fine now that Ned seems to be exhibiting better self-control." Mitch had a gut-wrenching sensation as he pictured his young client in a heavily sedated state. He thought fast.

"Would it be helpful for me to contact Dr. Script? I would be glad to share with her the information about Ned that I have gathered from the school and my sessions with him." His parents were likely to have emphasized their concerns, without any positive feedback, about Ned in the psychiatrist's office.

As is typical in such cases, Mrs. Kopresis self-righteously believed that each of her steps to help her poor son was a correct one. "Sure, that would be fine. The more his doctors know about Ned's problems, the better."

Mitch arranged to send Ned's parents a consent form to enable him legally and ethically to exchange information with the psychiatrist. Unfortunately, he knew too well that his diagnosis of Factitious Disorder Imposed on Another, indicating a need to treat the parents, not the child, may well be ignored. And even if Dr. Script somehow managed to agree with him, it would only drive Mr. and Mrs. Kopresis to take Ned elsewhere for treatment.

Mitch was feeling demoralized when a knock on the door suggested that Mr. Opus had arrived for his appointment. "Good afternoon, Ed," welcomed a tired, deflated Mitch, with as much warmth as he could muster.

"Greetings, Dr. Treasure!" His enthusiastically good mood caught Mitch by surprise.

"You seem pretty chipper today, Ed. How have things been going for you?"

"Just peachy. Work is good, my wife and I are getting along famously, and our love life has never been better."

"Why, I must say that is good to hear. Why this improvement? What have you done to get things going so well?"

"I've been following your advice, Doc."

"You mean, I hope, that you have been following through with some of the ideas that *you* have come up with during our discussions."

"Yeah, whatever. All I know is that Electra and I are talking more, telling how we feel about one another, and doing more things together.

My telling her how I really feel about erotic experiences has taken the frequency and intensity of our romantic interludes to new heights."

"That's just great, Ed," Mitch praised warmly. "It sounds as though better marital communication has done the trick after all."

"Yes, I guess you could say that. Of course, some well-placed choco-lates, a few floral bouquets, occasional glasses of wine, restaurant dining, flattery, assorted gifts, her favorite mood music, and our enrollment in dance and massage classes haven't hurt, either."

"Holy holism! You've been pretty thorough, Ed, doing more than I could possibly have brainstormed with you."

"Yes, but you got me started, Doc. You're okay."

And that ended another rollercoaster week of psychotherapy for Mitch.

While Mitch and Max were wrapping up their work weeks and looking forward to the relatively relaxed pace of the next couple of days, Claude and his inner circle of cronies were gearing up for a busy weekend. They convened at a Rochester restaurant named "Something Fishy" to consume some seafood and put the finishing touches on a malicious plot.

"Claude, are you sure that this is the time and place for us to act?" inquired Tony. "That golf course is going to be patrolled by plenty of police." Bart and Ernie gestured that they shared Tony's concern.

"Yes, so the cops will not suspect that we have the balls to attack then and there. And it's too good of an opportunity to miss. Where else are we going to find so many of those pseudo-religious leaders running about, engaging in the folly that helps to bring down our people and nation? A charity golf tournament to honor a blasphemous reverend, collecting money to give to would-be clergy and golfers—it's maddening!"

"But how are we going to pull this off?" asked Tony's new part-ner, Billy. "On what plan have you decided, based on our scouting of the course?"

"I agree that it would be foolhardy to return to the scene of our previous activities. Even when they are preoccupied by their silly game, some of those folks might be wary of that area of the golf course. Police might even be staked out there. So, I have picked an alternate site, a heavily forested spot that gives us similar cover and an escape route. I also think that it's a place in which players may have let down their guards."

Bart ventured to ask, "Could we shoot more than one? There will be so many targets."

"You betcha," affirmed Claude. "Two or three quick shots, then skedaddle."

Drinking somewhat more alcohol than usual, the fivesome mapped out details for their intended misdeeds.

Max and Mitch were glad to be at the dojo on Friday for the special seminar with a visiting sensei, Jethro Masakatsu. The Japanese-American master from San Francisco was on a tour of aikido schools around the East Coast. His long-time friendship with the local sensei, Mr. Kikai, brought him to the Rochester area. Mitch and Max, naturally, were going to have to miss his Saturday classes due to the charity tournament at Rolling Greens, but at least they could partake of the practices that evening and on Sunday morning. Besides, since this was the regularly scheduled time for the advanced class, they were hopeful that Masakatsu Sensei would involve them in some particularly worthwhile activities on this occasion.

After the customary ritual of opening class, and Kikai Sensei's cordial introduction of his friend before turning over instruction to him, Mr. Masakatsu led the students through a welcome blend of routine and unaccustomed stretching exercises. He incorporated some yoga, *tai chi chuan*, and calisthenics into the warm-up activities. He even put in a good word for cross-training. He repeated their teacher's oft-used adage that strength is not of primary importance, yet is virtuous, and then expanded that message by saying that aikido training alone is not a path to well-being; it is wise to exercise in various ways, eat nutritiously, get ample rest, and seek both vocational and interpersonal satisfaction. Max and Mitch felt in sync with the vibes coming from their guest instructor. "*Ukemi*," he commanded succinctly when their warm-ups were completed. The group of about two dozen students formed a single line at one edge of the mats, then did right shoulder rolls in a counter-clockwise half-circle around the perimeter of the padded area. Getting up more or less dizzily, most of them pounded their heels into the floor to reestablish a sense of equilibrium. They reversed themselves by doing a clockwise-directed series of left shoulder rolls, followed by back rolls on alternating shoulders. "Four lines," requested Masakatsu Sensei. "Run and roll." Each wave of students trotted halfway across the mat area before flinging themselves into a forward roll, coming up smoothly to a balanced standing position before proceeding to the opposite end of the room. They repeated the sequence five more times.

"Get *bokkens*." His terse speech contained more than a trace of Japanese accent.

The advanced students bowed off the mat en route to their personal weapons bags in order to fetch their wooden swords. Relative beginners, there for the seminar, armed themselves from the rack of extra *bokkens* on the far wall of the dojo.

"Our weapons are not for aggression or violence of any kind." Masakatsu Sensei stated the obvious for the benefit of the novices and spectators at the workshop. "They are training tools. We swing *bokken* to help us learn aikido techniques and to help us with other activities in our daily lives." Max wondered what applications he had in mind.

"Whether you are an advanced or beginning student, I hope that you find it helpful to review how to cut with *bokken*."

He proceeded to demonstrate proper form, emphasizing soft grip and harmony with the force of gravity. He explained how relaxation breeds power. As the *bokken* begins to drop from its elevated, vertical, preparatory position, the wrists subtly cock. Potential energy is gradually stored as the sword continues to fall vertically, and then force is powerfully unleashed as the sword approaches its target and snaps toward it into a near-horizontal position with the tip at throat level.

"So it is with baseball, golf, tennis, and hockey," Masakatsu Sensei explained. "Power is generated by creating drag, by moving the body and arms toward the target before the wrists snap at the last second." He demonstrated again with his *bokken*, first as though swinging a baseball bat and secondly on the plane of a golf swing. "Focused force is achieved through centeredness and relaxation."

Max did not care if others in the room noticed his beaming face, his rapt attention, and his sense of affirmation as Sensei spoke his language. It was an epiphany for Max: More than any other aspect of aikido training, perhaps the principles and feel of swinging *bokken* could best transfer competence and consistency to his golf game.

XIII

IT'S WINNING TIME

SATURDAY DAWNED WITH THE PROMISE OF BRIGHT SUNSHINE and high late-June temperatures. The humidity of early summer had diminished somewhat, but it was still going to be muggy. If any of the players had been torn between walking or riding around Rolling Greens, they were likely to choose golf carts for the day's excursion. Not so for Max and Mitch. They were confirmed walkers who usually tried to choose like-minded playing partners. Father Mulligan and Rabbi Greene, as physically fit as their ages and busy spiritual pursuits allowed them to be, would do nicely.

The tournament to honor the memory of the popular Reverend Eagleton was a well-organized affair. His widow and devoted parishioners had intentionally scheduled the event seven weeks after his untimely passing in order to make sure that it was put together effectively. The latter also wanted to enable the former to have plenty of time to move through part of the grieving process. The chairperson of the reverend's church board of directors, Ralph Steeple, who coincidentally had been playing with Mr. Eagleton on the day of his demise, was the official director of the tournament. Non-golfing members of the Wholly Holy Christian Academy (WHCA), along with some supervisors of the Junior Golf Association (JGA), staffed the various registration and service tables for the event. Rolling Greens was selected as the site of the affair since it was centrally located, south of Rochester, and not too distant from Buffalo, Syracuse, Binghamton, and other areas of Upstate New York.

The entry fee covered greens fees, lunch, prizes, and most importantly, contributions to the two main charities, the WHCA and JGA, along with two more designated charities: the National Audubon Society (since Reverend Eagleton often said, "Life is for the birds") and the American Red Cross. Personal, corporate, and church donations enhanced the charitable funding. The local church diocese, together with some regional golf courses, kicked in money to provide each participant with a sleeve of golf balls and a bag of tees. As host of the event, Rolling Greens profited indirectly, via advertising, from this act of generosity by giving away lightweight jackets and towels with its logo printed on them. Prizes—in the form of plaques and trophies along with merchandise and cash certificates from the pro shop—were to be awarded in a complicated array of competitions. There were separate divisions for men and women, individuals and teams, clergy and laypersons, and gross and net scores. Closest shots to the pin on the par-3 sixth and seventeenth holes, longest drives on numbers one and eighteen, and fewest putts for the round would also be honored. So, good-naturedly, would the highest score of the day. Perhaps ironically, as a professional and the only player with the legal and ethical right to accept tangible reward for playing well, Max was the sole participant to be excluded from the competitions because of his professional playing status.

Mitch, because he was paired with Max, who was ineligible as a teammate, entered only the individual contest. Their playing companions, Rabbi Greene and Father Mulligan, formed an interdenominational partnership. They placed some wagers on the side—mainly with good deeds rather than money at stake—with some of their colleagues. For instance, they had guest sermons on the line with Father Golfinski and Rabbi Winestain. Pastor Pintender and Reverend Lagger offered to co-host an interfaith luncheon if they lost; Father Mulligan and Rabbi Greene put up a joint yard sale to match the offer. As Max witnessed the betting intensify, and the stakes increase, he was not surprised to overhear some prayers on the first tee. Some even muttered heavenly offerings while genuflecting in the process of plucking their golf balls out of the holes on the practice green.

"Some of these folks are going to experience some holy doldrums if they play poorly on these holey grounds today," Max commented to Mitch as they started practice swinging on the first tee.

"Yes, the pressure is on. But not for you and me, partner. I'm just psyched to play on this day of gorgeous weather."

"What's your pleasure, Dr. Treasure?" inquired the approaching rabbi. "Would you gentlemen care to lead off or go second?"

"Let's flip a tee to see," responded Mitch. The divine duo won the toss.

"Since we're in this up to our necks already, how about a friendly wager with you guys too?" ventured Father Mulligan

"What do you have in mind?" Max asked.

"If we win, you two have to come to our church and synagogue, respectively, to deliver brief inspirational messages to our Sunday School classes."

"And if we win?" Mitch queried with a smile.

"We buy you each a soft drink."

Max jumped in. "Hey, wait one minute there, Father. It is your belief that our time is worth no more than the cost of a soda pop?"

"Well, we were hoping . . ." he said, with a wink at the attentively amused rabbi.

"Let's see. What would be a fair exchange?" Mitch asked himself as much as the others.

"Time for time," Max mused. "How about your caddying for us for nine holes some Saturday?"

"It's a deal," said the confident clergymen in unison.

Their friendly match was an uneven affair. Even with the strokes that Max and Mitch gave them, the rabbi and priest were outgunned from the start. Coupling his mental image and feel of swinging the

wooden sword with his usual swing keys, Max hit the ball consistently straight and far. As was often the case in the aftermath of an aikido class the preceding evening, Mitch felt centered and relaxed that morning. He, too, played one of his best rounds of the season. In their game of high-low, the laymen were ten points ahead of their pious brethren by the end of the front nine.

At the snack shack between the ninth green and the tenth tee, they caught up with the foursome in front of them.

"How are you hitting today, Sister Rotini?" Max asked.

"Like a pro," she replied. "Sister Stroker and I had a net best-ball score of, what, Sister, two under par? We shot thirty-four, right?"

"Precisely, Sister," affirmed her playing partner. These two nuns were like the *yin* and *yang* of the tournament field. Sister Rotini was young, pretty, perky, and petite. Sister Stroker, likewise a teacher at Bishop Niblick High School, was an enormous middle-aged woman with a no-nonsense demeanor. Max imagined the two of them in their respective classrooms, the former gaining the attention of her English students because of her attractiveness and sweet disposition, and the latter commanding respect in her mathematics classes because of her imposing presence. In the opinion of the school's principal, Sister Pedagodge, with whom Max had played golf on two occasions, both were well-liked by their students.

"Way to go!" Max encouraged.

"I suppose that you young lions are burning up the course today," said another member of their foursome, Pastor Pitchmun.

Father Mulligan preempted any reply by Max or Mitch. "You can see the steam rising from the preceding fairways and greens. These gentlemen are too hot to handle."

"What was your best-ball score, if I may ask?" inquired Sister Rotini.

Max answered, "Well, it doesn't count in the tournament, and we're only halfway, so I really don't—"

"Thirty, and that is with only one handicap stroke provided by the good Dr. Treasure," jumped in Rabbi Greene.

"Holy Mother of Pearl! That's smokin'," said the staid Sister Stroker. Yes, Max could now understand how her students enjoy their animated teacher.

As they stood watching the sisters and their companions tee off on the back nine, the trailing group stepped up to the snack shack just behind Max's foursome. Father Mulligan strode back to confer with his colleague, Father Spoonini, the priest at a cathedral in Buffalo. Rabbi Birdman, with hard-boiled egg in one hand and lemonade in the other, walked up to exchange pleasantries with Rabbi Greene.

"God may be on our side," Max overheard the visiting rabbi say, "but He hasn't told me how to read these greens. I must have taken two dozen putts already."

"When in doubt, go right at them," advised Rabbi Greene. "Better yet, I'd like to introduce you to the pro here, Max Azure. Max, this is Rabbi Birdman from Niagara Falls."

After they shook hands, Max added to the advice about putting. "As Rabbi Greene says, hit your putts straight and firm most of the time. But you'll notice that many putts break toward that telecommunications tower on yonder hill."

"Are they pulled there by electromagnetic forces?" quipped the rabbi.

"I haven't considered that hypothesis. But I'm sure that the prevailing winds and slopes, along with the grain, tend to go that way."

Mitch beckoned Max to meet another member of the group playing behind them. "Max, I'd like you to meet the new Chaplain of Confluence College, Walter Wedger. Chaplain, this is Max Azure, the golf pro among us."

They exchanged handshakes. "Welcome to Ebbinflo and to Rolling Greens," Max said. "How do you like it here so far?"

"Having moved from Colorado, I must say that the climate and terrain are distinctly different but equally enjoyable. The golf course is plush and challenging. And the people here have been every bit as nice as those at USC."

"You came from the University of Southern Colorado?" Max exclaimed. "That's where I got my master's degree in golf course management."

"That's cool," responded the chaplain. "Let's compare notes about Pueblo and vicinity."

"It'll have to be later, guys, because the tenth fairway is wide open and awaiting our drives," interrupted Mitch.

The incoming nine went pretty much as did the outgoing one. Humor and good will prevailed in the featured foursome, despite the tournament atmosphere and the fact that Mitch and Max were slaying the rabbi and priest in their high-low match. Max suffered only a couple of lapses in concentration, but they led only to one bogey and one missed birdie putt. He was five under par by the time they reached the seventeenth tee. Mitch, a four-handicapper, stood at three-over. Father Mulligan and Rabbi Greene, although trailing dramatically in their side match, were actually playing their usual games, just slightly above their handicaps.

Max led off with a six-iron on the lengthy par-3. His shot just barely carried the 180 yards to the front edge of the green, released, and rolled up to within twenty feet of the hole. Mitch, in the competition to hit closest to the pin, mimicked Max's shot but with a five-iron. His lower trajectory enabled the ball to roll farther once it hit the green. It looked close. Rabbi Greene pulled a seven-wood shot to the left edge of the green while Father Mulligan reached the left front apron with his three-iron. They had all safely avoided the creek that wound its way around the right side of the green.

Mitch was just starting the process of measuring the distance of his shot from the hole, in order to compare it to the current leader's distance, when the guys heard cries go up from the tee behind them. A glance in that direction showed four men either hitting the ground or running for cover. Only because of their previous encounter with this situation did Mitch and Max immediately recognize what was happening. With putters in hand, they dashed for the forest that lined the left side of the hole. A slight rustling there indicated that they were on target for their objective; they did not hesitate to realize that the tables, or weapons, could quickly turn so as to make them the quarry. Thank goodness for quick reflexes! Max saw a golf ball streaking at him and raised his putter just in the nick of time. *Ping!* went the ball off the face of his club, just right of his own face. The recoil knocked his putter backwards almost to the ground, but he held onto it. Mitch hit the deck. But he wasn't safe there. A projectile flew just over his head and glanced off his derriere. "Ow!" he yelped.

As if on cue by a director of some bizarre movie, Mitch and Max started doing *ukemi*, forward shoulder rolls, in a zig-zag pattern. Actually, there was no pattern. They just started doing rolls in seemingly random directions—some to one side or the other, and some obliquely toward the woods—in an evasive manner, all the while still clutching their putters. Then Max caught a glimpse of their assailants, men dressed in camouflage uniforms and aiming some tubes—each looked like a cross between a military bazooka and a toy burp gun—at him. He lunged into a roll to his left and felt another golf ball nick his shoe.

Max vaguely heard male shouts for help, presumably emanating from the seventeenth tee, but they were merely on the edge of his consciousness because he was absorbed in his actions. He did, however, make out the words, "Let's scram," from the trees ahead. In the next instant, another ball streaked out at Mitch. His dive to his right effectively protected his vital parts, but his rear end was momentarily elevated as he rolled. The "whoosh" of another tangential hit to his tush elicited a moan. "Ooh!" Since the intense rustling in the undergrowth ahead suggested that their tormentors were taking off, Max turned his attention to Mitch.

"Are you okay, buddy?"

"My gluteus maximus is singing the blues. Both buns—yowch, that stings! But yeah, I'm all right."

"Hold onto your putter. Let's go get 'em."

Max stood up and moved, still warily looking ahead, toward the edge of the forest. Mitch groaned audibly as he rose and then started off in a limp, but he gradually lengthened his stride. What the heck were they doing, Max thought, as he cautiously jogged, not ran, forward. Surely the police would soon give pursuit, and this was a job for them, not for a golf pro and a psychologist. He and Mitch must be taking their study of aikido too seriously, Max thought, exceeding its tenet of "loving protection of all living things." They were chasing trouble.

They slowed at the edge of the woods, spotted the culprits fleeing in the distance up ahead, and plunged into the trees. Now feeling less threat from the escaping men, Max sped up. Mitch did his best to do likewise, but his bruised rump slowed him down. Max surged ahead. It's amazing how quickly the mind works, he thought, enabling you to flash upon many ideas in a short span of time, even when you are engrossed in an activity. Among other things, Max wished that his putter were a machete with which to chop through the undergrowth between him and the bad guys, and to defend himself if and when he caught up with them. He marveled at how rapidly his eyes read the scene before him and guided every footfall over challenging terrain. He wondered what Kikai Sensei would do in this situation. He hoped that Rabbi Birdman, Father Spoonini, and their playing partners were uninjured back on the tee. He felt grateful for the cross-training that gave him the stamina to be running through the woods. Max even recalled Magic Johnson of the Los Angeles Lakers with his oft-expressed statement, "It's winnin' time," as a game neared its climactic finish. Then reality interrupted his reverie.

Max rushed into a little clearing and saw one of those weird guns aiming straight at him from a bush ahead. As the white projectile exploded from its muzzle, his brain flashed on a childhood scene: sometimes, when a snowball is thrown at your face, the best defense is neither to duck nor dodge but simply to catch it; sometimes, there is even enough of it left to throw back at your assailant. It was a bad idea here, though. Max raised a hand and ducked simultaneously. The ball nicked the middle fingertip of his golf-gloved left hand. Even the glancing blow was forceful enough to drive his hand backwards. He couldn't help but let out a yelp.

A louder cry emanated from Mitch as he leaped unsteadily into the clearing with a *kiai*, the shout typical of karate and kung fu practitioners that is intended to release one's maximal energy and intimidate an opponent. It was rapidly followed by, "Oh, no!" as Mitch spied the second golf ball bazooka aiming at him. This time, his evasive maneuver—simply rolling backwards—was effective. The groan Max heard was due to Mitch's landing on his sore buttocks, not a fresh wound. Max and Mitch scrambled backwards into the cover of undergrowth, and each stood behind a tree.

Mitch and Max looked at one another in bewilderment. Under normal circumstances, no one in his right mind would attack anyone on a golf course because one's bag of golf clubs makes a darn good set of defensive weapons. Their sense of security in this case, however, surely had been shaken. Thank goodness those golf ball cannons appeared to be only single-shot models that needed cocking and reloading between rounds—Mitch and Max had time to decide between fight and flight.

Peering around their trees, Max and Mitch saw signs of renewed departure by the malefactors. Max pointed to suggest that Mitch circle the clearing to his right, and that he would take the left perimeter. Their reasoning skills still overshadowed by the thrill of the chase, they started running toward the peril again.

Max heard sirens in the distance. Were they heading toward them, perhaps converging on a point on the trail ahead? He hoped so. He only imagined that he heard helicopters gyrating overhead to rescue the would-be heroes, Mitch and him.

Staying wide of, but presumably parallel to, the path taken by the attackers, Max ran as fast as the forested conditions would allow. After a minute or two, he started to angle to his right and—holy smokes—came upon two guys immediately. A big guy swung his bazooka toward Max, but not before he had a chance to swing his putter. The "clang" of impact knocked the weapon from the guy's grasp but, alas, sent the head of Max's beloved putter flying as well. He retained his grip on what was now something like a lightweight sword, the steel shaft of his putter. As the other man threw a punch at him, Max swiveled aside and cut the putter shaft down upon his extended elbow. The man yowled in pain as he fell facedown onto the forest floor. But the big guy grabbed Max, not just by the shirt or arm, but in a potentially life-ending bear hug that pinned his arms to his body. He was as strong as he looked. His squeeze knocked the breath out of Max. But he did not panic, even as he saw the other guy lumber to his feet and begin to take aim with the fist of his uninjured arm. Fortunately for Max, this situation triggered his memory of another aikido maneuver that he had practiced enough times to make a part of himself. He extended his fingers forward, palms down, just enough to create an inch of space between the brute's arms and Max's chest. He then slid downward and to his right, under the guy's arm, dropping his putter shaft in the process. As Max rose again, he cut his right palm down the big lug's elbow just enough to lead him off balance, then applied a painful forearm technique—*yonkyo*—with which he transported the guy straight into his advancing cohort. Max reflexively smiled when the fist intended for him impacted the giant's head instead. Retrieving his putter shaft, Max took a step back and pointed it at the two men who had stumbled into a position facing him a few feet away. Breathing very heavily, looking fully demoralized, they seemed to want no more action with Max, especially with the menacing manner in which he steadily directed his "sword" at their throats.

Mitch soon arrived on the scene. He quickly kicked the fallen golf ball "gun" aside, well out of anyone's reach. Then, mirroring Max, he pointed his still-intact putter at the two perpetrators. "You look pretty fearsome there, buddy," he panted.

"It's putter power, pal," Max retorted. They allowed themselves a smile. Their two captives did not share their amusement. Max blinked as he looked from one perpetrator to the other. "Are you two brothers?" It was Bart, or his fraternal twin, Ernie, who muttered, "Yeah."

Figuring that two captives were better than none, and not wanting to face any more golf balls rocketing at themselves, Max and Mitch moved their entourage back in the direction from which they had come. Their putters, particularly the sharp-ended one, kept their marching companions on course. Mitch carried their two weapons, with considerable strain, in his gloved hand alone. He had some notion about not wanting to disturb any fingerprints that may have been on them. He added the support of his right hand when Max mentioned that the accompanying culprits could provide all the fingerprints that the police might need.

They trekked back to the seventeenth hole, now bustling with police and emergency medical personnel, with their malevolent hiking partners. Detective Southworth was himself on hand to take custody of the offenders. Mitch was glad to be relieved of the awkward weapons, though he did not seek physical relief in the form of a seat since his keister was too tender. He sheepishly accepted a brief medical examination that only confirmed that he had a bruised backside. Rabbi Birdman had been less fortunate. Expecting nothing, his reflexes slowed by age and his rather sedentary lifestyle, he had received a severe blow from, of all things, a Bettergolf Birdieball. The rabbi was unconscious and bleeding from his head but was getting medical attention. The other member of the rabbi's foursome who was struck by a ball was more fortunate. Pastor Flange appeared to have a shoulder injury, possibly a broken clavicle. It wasn't that he had taken cover from the shot that arrived almost simultaneously with the one that struck the rabbi; he was just fortunate to have been shot by a lesser marksman. The scope that was attached to each golf ball gun went a long way toward explaining its accuracy.

It wasn't until they returned to the clubhouse that Max and Mitch found out that a second pair of homicidal maniacs were also in custody. The sirens they had heard from the forest had indeed indicated that a swarm of law enforcement officers were closing in on the vicinity. The culprits had cleverly parked their well-stocked van in the cover of woods the night before the tournament and kept themselves camouflaged until the time to strike. The smattering of undercover police officers playing in the golf tournament, and the few patrol cars cruising the area, had been insufficient to detect and prevent the day's tragedy. But the police were more than ready to stop the villains' escape. The fleeing pair safely reached their vehicle, but law officers nabbed them before they could get the engine started. They wisely felt that their single-shot golf ball cannons were outmatched by police firearms and surrendered peacefully. They, like the two scoundrels whom Mitch and Max had apprehended, were likely destined to spend many future years behind bars, hopefully apart from their partners in crime.

Detective Southworth walked up to Max and Mitch in the clubhouse where they were recuperating from their ordeal by nursing a couple of lagers. Max was seated at a barstool while, naturally, Mitch merely leaned on one.

"You guys. Me oh my. You did it again."

Mitch said, "Actually, it was Max who got all the action and deserves the credit this time."

"Is that so? Well, I've been wondering. Are you sure you're not cops, maybe FBI or some other agency I'm not supposed to know about?"

"No way, and we plan never to act like police officers again," Max said. "It's your job, and you can have it."

"I'm not so sure about that," replied the detective. "I mean, I know that it's my job, but it seems that you guys just can't resist mixing it up with bogeymen."

"Let's just say that we often try to do the right thing, and we've read too many crime novels," said Mitch, "but we hope to high heaven that you'll now get to the bottom of this thing. Golf courses are supposed to be havens of peace and safety, not martial arts training grounds."

"Hallelujah. We'll round up the ringleaders, all right. That big guy you captured isn't as mentally tough as the other big oaf you brought into custody previously. He's already spouting out prayers, whining that God made him do it, and throwing around at least the first names of some of his murderous brethren. And if he doesn't crack, one of the other three will."

"I don't suppose that we could offer you some liquid refreshment, Detective," Max proposed.

"I'd have ginger ale—it's supposed to make your hands feel thinner for a better grip on the golf club, I hear—but I'll have to pass because I must get back to work. I just stopped by to thank you guys for all of your help, and to give you this souvenir, Dr. Treasure." He handed Mitch a shiny new Whizbang 90 golf ball. "We found this on the seventeenth, close to where you reportedly took a dive. It's practically new, been hit only once, and almost got a hole in one, I understand."

"Very funny," responded Mitch in unison with Max's laughter.

XIV

ENCORE

THE HOLY HELP CAPTIVES DID NOT SPILL THE BEANS AFTER ALL. Big Bart may have started blathering about God's will and the first names of some of his compatriots. But when he caught a pinch from his little brother, Ernie, and a glimpse of Tony's tight-lipped gesture toward him, he clammed up. After their initial feelings of frustration and anger at having been apprehended subsided, three of the four felt a return to self-righteousness and loyalty to their organization. Claude, and his message, commanded allegiance. They respected their oaths of silence due not only to their fear that they might evoke anger and revenge from Claude, but also to their belief that the Lord's wrath would be upon them if they betrayed Him.

Billy, who had experienced less indoctrination into the beliefs of HH, likewise honored his vow of loyalty. He wondered guiltily what had compelled him to get mixed up in this nasty business in the first place. Buried in a blend of shame and self-punishment, Billy decided that the right thing to do was to play out this chapter of his life to whatever bitter conclusion it might reach. Feeling that he had only himself to blame for his predicament, he refused to disclose the names of Claude and his comrades to the legal authorities.

Law enforcement officers exerted as much pressure on the captured zealots as they could. They felt surprised and madly frustrated by the uncooperative silence with which they were met. They did, however, manage to follow a trail from some of their captives to two other members of HH: Billy's liaison, Bruce, and JD's friend, Mike. The former seemed genuinely dull-witted and in the dark about how to locate the leadership or headquarters of the organization. Mike was a master of the adolescent arts of passive resistance and oppositional behavior; he met police queries first with sullen silence and then with outbursts of misleading information. It would take time for the detectives to piece together the grains of truth in Mike's disclosure and to find any useful tracks to the head of HH.

Claude, for his part, experienced a mixture of negative thoughts and emotions in the wake of the capture of his most prized allies and assassins. He cursed himself for misjudging the situation at Rolling Greens, second-guessing that the attack there had been either erroneously planned or altogether ill-advised. He grieved the loss of his most trusted lieutenants. He felt worried about their fates as well as the future power of HH. As the hours and days passed after the setback, however, another emotion gained preeminence in Claude's thinking: hatred.

He had taken it as a stroke of bad luck when those two golfers had managed to capture Frank during the botched attempt to slay Father Mulligan. But twice was no mere coincidence. Those guys, for thwarting him on two occasions, deserved Claude's rage. In his private, delusional consultations with his image of the Divine Spirit, Claude gained affirmation that his desire for revenge was justified. As he thought about what members of HH could best replace his two strike teams, he thought also that their first targets should be those meddling golfers—one of whom he already knew all too well. If necessary, Claude himself would carry out the will of the Lord against them.

It took several days before Max and Mitch felt golf-worthy again. Regions of Mitch's buttocks turned various shades of blue, purple, and yellow, superficially revealing the soreness that stiffened and curtailed his movements. Max felt that he had gotten through the exchange with the bad guys unscathed, but the high-velocity contact of the golf ball with the middle finger of his left hand caused not only the loss of that fingernail, but also the inability to grasp a golf club with sufficient authority to control it.

His capacity to demonstrate good golf had been impaired temporarily, but Max could still carry on his livelihood as a teaching professional. Sister Rotini took a lesson and gave a lesson; Max enhanced her ability to pitch and run shots close to the pin from edges of greens, and she reminded him that compassion and forgiveness are divine states of mind that ease traumatic memories of violence into the background of one's life. Roger returned to practice his impulsive approach to golf, though he behaved better than he had previously; he paid some attention to Max's modeling and instruction, still swinging forcefully but with enough control to hit some straight shots. Eleanor Wholesome, near the other end of the age spectrum, had a tune-up to confirm that her timeless golf game kept on ticking properly. Larry Bogart kept up his habit of meeting periodically with Max, working to improve his balance and accuracy on long shots. He had difficulty keeping his head still, and hence his center of balance, so inconsistency reigned. Bogey was making solid contact on most shots, but his directionality was too often warped. Max thought of Sister Rotini as he preached the virtues of self-compassion and self-forgiveness to the agitated Bogey. After that lesson, Max was in for a pleasant jolt. Whom should he see getting out of his car at the golf club parking lot but his fellow aikidoist, Theodore Seidokai.

"Theodore, fancy seeing you here," greeted Max.

"Yes, this is new territory for me," said the soft-spoken assistant instructor. "Believe it or not, I have come to arrange to take golf lessons from you."

"Hey, that's cool. What has made you want to take up golf? And how are you going to fit in this time-consuming game with your graduate studies and responsibilities as a cellist?" Max knew that Theodore was going to the Eastman School of Music part time in pursuit of a doctorate, played for the Rochester Concert Orchestra, and taught a number of private students on the side.

"Golf has intrigued me for many years. You are aware, I'm sure, of the passion for the game in my native Japan. I have always sensed its kinship with aikido. That relationship, made explicit by you over the several years we have trained together, and by Masakatsu Sensei in his recent seminar, piqued my interest. As for time . . . who knows?" He threw up his hands and eyebrows simultaneously.

"Well, welcome to Rolling Greens. Let's step into the pro shop to schedule a time. Do you have golf clubs?"

"Yes, my uncle's old set."

Uh oh, thought Max. Technology had probably passed him by. Modern golf clubs hold huge advantages over those of the previous generation. But, knowing Theodore's dedication to detail and capacity for graceful yet powerful movement, he'd probably pick up the basics in no time flat.

They arranged to get together weekly for the next month. Then Max invited Theodore to help himself to practice on the putting green. Not only did it cost nothing; it was also a helpful strategy to start a novice such as Theodore with the small, refined activity of putting. It was in harmony with his personal style, not to mention that putting accounts for nearly half the strokes taken by the average golfer. On his way to the practice tee to meet with his final student of the day, Max spotted Theodore as he lined up putts, using an old Ace putter with a pitted face, with the exacting approach with which he taught lessons in the dojo.

Whack! "That ball must have gone two hundred seventy yards on the fly," gushed Wayne Windham.

"That's a good guess, Wayne," Max concurred. "Your big swing can power some big-time drives. How have you been scoring lately?"

Wayne teed up another range ball and addressed it before responding. "About the same as usual, Max." He swung and knocked the ball a long distance—but this time it arced so far to the right, and off the practice range, that they could not see it land. "In fact, very much like that. I follow a straight shot with a wild one."

"But Wayne, after all, you were talking both before and after that swing," Max soothed. "Do you distract yourself on the course like that?"

"Yes, probably." He hit another, this one a high fade that stayed within view.

"If you talk in the act of swinging, not only will you hit inconsistently, hit too quickly, and ignore your pre-shot routine," Max advised, "but notice your finish. On both of those shots, you blocked out your hips so badly, and over-swung so much, that you ended up on your toes."

"I *am* off-balance, aren't I?" he admitted, seeming to notice it for the first time.

Max thought that Wayne could be his golf student for life, given the slowness with which he came to understand and adopt changes for the better. But Max stuck sincerely to his goal of helping his golf pupils learn to play better independently, with diminishing need for lessons. Wayne needed patient reminders. "Remember early in the summer when we reviewed your swing keys?"

Wayne recalled and recited some. He lined up as he addressed the next ball, sighed as he assumed a balanced posture, and popped up the ball a short distance but straight ahead.

"Wayne, I may have detected something in your swing that could help you. You obviously have a long arc, thanks to your height, and nothing feels better than knocking a golf ball a long distance. But I believe that a subtle left elbow bend has crept into your swing. Please try a somewhat shorter backswing, letting your energy flow through your left arm to keep it straight. After a little pause at that point of transition before your downswing, you may cut loose and see what happens."

What happened was a series of straight shots. "Holy howitzer! Max, you're a genius. I haven't hit the ball that well for as far back as I can remember."

"A genius I'm not. We all know that we're supposed to keep the arm straight during the backswing. It just took me a while to catch you in the act of violating that rule. Besides, this is just the practice range. You'll want to hit more balls, play some rounds, and remind yourself of those swing keys to keep your arm straight and your swing smooth."

Feeling gratified that he had prompted bits of progress in some of his students that day, Max decided to linger on the lesson tee to see how his own grip and swing were progressing. Little did he know that Wayne, his early-evening student, had chosen to stay in the vicinity as well, under cover of some thickets not far from the practice range. His target practice this time, however, was not hitting drives toward a fairway. Rather, he had his sights set on Max. His tubular, compressed-air golf ball projector was cocked and loaded. Wayne was new at wielding the weapon, but he had the strength to hold it steady as he used the scope to zero in on Max's steady head.

Just as Wayne began to squeeze the trigger, the words "Max, get down!" were shouted. Wayne reacted by easing up, withdrawing the weapon, and getting ready to move to his car. Too late. Four officers emerged from within and around the bushes, pistols drawn. In the meantime, Max, lying on the turf, saw a pair of shoes progressing toward him. He glanced upward. "Detective Southworth! What's going on? What are you doing here?"

"I'm just following up a hunch and practicing a well-worn maxim. If you look behind you, you'll see a tall gentleman being apprehended while he was preparing to kill you. Vengeance against you was my hunch. The maxim has to do with villains often returning to the scenes of their crimes."

"Holy moly, it's Wayne! Really? Trying to kill me?"

"That's not a putter he was aiming at you."

Mitch shared Max's shock that one of his favorite, long-time golf students had not only been involved with HH all along, but had eventually brought himself to turn against Max with deadly force. It remained unclear whether or not Wayne was the mastermind of the HH organization, but his treachery was deeply upsetting to Max. It made Mitch wonder what darkness lay in the hearts of some of his clients—people already recognized as having mental health issues, some with irrational thinking that could be attracted to the beliefs of a fanatical and dangerous cult.

The day after Max's close call with death, Mitch continued treatment of Leonard Tourette, helping the man gradually to gain control of some of his nervous mannerisms. Haley could not improve much, given her schizophrenic condition, but she experienced some episodes of emotional support and social guidance with Mitch. JD's attendance continued to be hit or miss, depending on his attitude and interpersonal distractions. Si Clothymik's mood likewise varied, sometimes featuring some dark and angry thinking, though he usually arrived at Mitch's punctually for his appointments. As Mitch predicted, Ned Kopresis dropped by the wayside; his mother wanted him treated, though not improved, for the range of ailments she imagined him to have.

Mitch, as usual, approached his mid-afternoon client with thoughtfulness about how their counseling session could best be conducted. He wished to help Hank become a competent individual. Talk therapy alone seemed unlikely to do the trick. Enveloped in self-doubt and anxiety, with a rich history of ineffectual behavior, Hank appeared unable to become self-sufficient. With his episodic damaging of property or engaging in self-injurious behavior, he was not about to earn the trust of significant others—such as a boss or landlord. Hank needed experiential learning. After asking about whether or not Hank had yet begun his vocational assessment, Mitch planned to take him for a walk around town in order to practice career exploration and social skills more directly than he could do in his office.

He had started his vocational evaluation, all right. Mitch learned this not from Hank but from the woman who accompanied him to the counseling session.

"Hi, I'm Val Paksil." The bespectacled woman, probably in the same age range as Mitch, introduced herself. She stood at least as tall as Hank and only a half-head shorter than Mitch. She wore a beige business suit under her tidy short brown hair. She struck Mitch as well-groomed and authoritative, if not a trifle imposing, to the clientele whom she oversaw.

"Ah, Hank's caseworker. Welcome. Thanks for bringing Hank." Mitch felt willing and ready to scrap his session plan for an off-the-cuff discussion with both Hank and Val.

"The reason I'm here is not all good," she responded. Hank walked in circles with his head down, wringing his hands and moaning softly to himself, as she said this.

Mitch, sensitive to Hank's obvious discomfort, spoke before Val could finish her thought.

"Yes, I'm glad you're here anyway. How about you, Hank? Is it okay to have Ms. Paxil join us, at least for a few minutes, today?"

"Yeah, I-I gu-gu-guess so." He ceased his pacing to run his hands through his straight reddish-brown hair. Mitch noticed a growing bald spot toward the left rear of his head.

"As I was saying—and I don't mean to put you on the spot, Hank—I came along to update you about how Hank is doing." Mitch sensed that she had been on the verge of saying something more critical before she took note of Hank's distress. Mitch was glad to see that she was sensitive to Hank's state of mind. "I took Hank to AEC—the Adult Education Center—yesterday."

Mitch motioned for his guests to be seated. They were. Then he prompted, "Yes?"

"Hank, why don't you tell Dr. Treasure a little about that place and your visit there." Mitch was pleased to hear her supportive tone.

He paused several seconds. "I-I-I-I liked the folks there. They t-t-tested me, then gave me a snack."

"Yes, they gave him some aptitude tests," she now addressed Mitch, "and Hank showed, as you and I suspected, that he has some keen abilities in the areas of spatial relationships, perceptual speed and accuracy, and quantitative reasoning skill."

"That's good news. Way to go, Hank!"

"Th-thanks, Dr. Treasure," said Hank, with a little smile and hint of eye contact with Mitch. He looked more relaxed.

"Between the testing and the snack, however," continued Val as Hank tensed again, "Hank excused himself to go to the restroom. Subsequently, some damage was discovered in there."

"Uh oh," said Mitch before he could catch himself.

Hank groaned then resumed his pacing and hand-wringing.

"Hank, it's okay," reassured Val. "You and I have been over this, and Dr. Treasure isn't shocked by it, are you?"

Mitch took the cue. "She's right, Hank. No sweat. Look at me for a second." Hank complied, for exactly that length of time. Mitch's quick wink had the desired effect. Hank collapsed into his usual chair with a sigh. He closed his eyes and rocked slowly from side to side.

"So, I just thought that you would want to know," continued Val, "that we followed through with your excellent suggestion. Hank showed some of his skills, but the AEC is presently unwilling to accept him for vocational training."

"Until they feel assured that there are no safety issues," Mitch surmised.

"Exactly. If and when he is ready, though, they could see him in their building trades program."

"So, another reason you're here today is to see how we can work together to help foster Hank's self-control?"

"Yes," she agreed with her first smile of the session. "Precisely."

The resulting co-therapy was a nice change of pace for Mitch. Haltingly, uncertain how to phrase things so as not to hurt Hank's feelings and not sure just what steps could be taken effectively, Mitch and Val brainstormed some strategies to help Hank curb his anxious and aggressive impulses. As a part of the team working on his own behalf, Hank willingly bought into the behavioral contract that resulted. Mitch felt guardedly optimistic as he bid the pair goodbye when the hour drew to a close.

Len was waiting outside the door. "Ah, Mr. T," greeted Mitch.

"Yes, 'tis I, Dr. T."

"You have no appointment with me."

"True, but please see me, temporarily."

Their lighthearted banter ended for the time being, Mitch bid Len to enter. He did so—without his knocking routine. Mitch grinned to himself.

"The reason I'm here, Doc, is just to let you know that I had a good weekend."

"That's always nice to hear."

Len needed no prompt to continue. "I went to that baseball game with Amelia. She intended to go along with me all along. And, man, was that game long! Rochester beat Hershey five to four in fourteen innings. The players moved as though their feet were mired in melted chocolate. And when the home team tied the game again, four-four, after Hershey had scored in the top of the twelfth, I was probably the only fan in the place who was disappointed. I thought the game would never end."

"Whoa, Len. I know that you find baseball to be a tediously long game. But weren't you enjoying your time with Amelia? Didn't you want your time with her stretched out?"

Len stretched and yawned. "You see? Just thinking about baseball makes me yawn! Yeah, I was glad to be there with her. In fact, we had a good time at the stadium. We talked throughout the whole game."

"I bet you did," interrupted Mitch.

"But I had plans to go somewhere with her after the game," carried on Len as though Mitch had said nothing, "to that new Spanish restaurant, La Paella Pretenciosa—so I was tired of waiting for the Slo-Mo Olympics to end. You know, a post-game margarita, then a little sangria with dinner . . ." Len actually lapsed into silence, gazing contentedly at the ceiling.

Mitch waited respectfully to allow Len a few seconds to enjoy his reminiscence. "So, you managed to mix sport with romance after all?"

"We didn't get intimate, if that's what you mean. But, yeah, it was a nice time. And guess what. Guess where we plan to go next?"

"To a fast-paced museum exhibition?"

"Oh, Dr. T, you've got my number. No, actually, we're heading to Buffalo this weekend to see professional wrestling."

"Hmmm. That's interesting. It's not the first place I'd think of for a date, but at least the energy level should be much to your liking."

Len got up to pace back and forth, throwing in a few pirouettes. He muttered some quasi-expletives under his breath—"schlep" and "fig-plucker" were barely audible. Mitch sighed with some contentment as he witnessed the transformation of Len's primary energy from useless anxiety to romantic excitement.

Most pleasurable for Mitch were his periodic contacts with a couple of Confluence College golf team members who lived in the vicinity and played at Rolling Greens during the summer months. He concluded his long day at the office with a six-hole stroll with two of those students. He thought about how stress continued to permeate the lives of golfers and non-golfers alike in Central New York. Perhaps the terrifying murderous clan had been corralled, but everyday challenges and friction competed with the joys of life for both Mitch's clients and Max's students. Golf only gradually took possession of Mitch's consciousness.

XV
LEARNING BY DOING

Melody's call reached Max's voicemail when she telephoned him on the first Tuesday in July.

"The first answer is 'No.' The second answer is, 'It depends on what *you* say.' The first question is, 'What is the most common manner in which puzzled people complete the phrase, I don't ____?' The second question is, 'Will Maxwell Azure be aware of why you've telephoned and how he can reach you in return?'"

"That's deep, Max. You're getting tricky. When you call me back, I'd like to talk about a novel idea: double dating. I think it would be fun for Mitch and Priscilla to go with us to Thrills & Spills Amusement Park this weekend. Let me know what you think. Bye, Sweetcakes."

The police were making progress, chipping away at the cultish crime ring. But the head of the dragon still eluded them. Wayne failed to meet the profile of the head of the gang of self-righteous assassins. And he kept his lips zipped, just as his captured brethren had likewise done. Tracing the movements and communications of Wayne, Billy, Bart, Ernie, and Tony, as well as the first captured culprit, Frank, had yielded hints at Holy Help meeting times and places, but nothing could be pinned down exactly. As a result, male and female members of the clergy were advised to put away their golf clubs for the season. The golfing public, as well, played with less frequency than usual.

Little did the authorities know that Wayne had been a founding member of the HH organization, a close compatriot of Claude's who chose to be called Mark instead of Wayne. At least that was the name that Billy blurted out when he saw Wayne being escorted to a cell near his own. As one of the leaders of the group, Wayne had opted not to be directly involved in the attacks on religious leaders. But he stepped up and decided to take a shot at his golf teacher; he valued Max as his instructor but found it unconscionable that Max had repeatedly thwarted and harmed HH. Claude had felt that Wayne, routinely close to unsuspecting Max, had the best chance of lowering the boom.

Claude was now beside himself with rage and consumed with thoughts of vengeance. Fewer members were attending HH meetings. His grip on those remaining was strong because of his charismatic presence, the power of the HH dogma, and the vulnerability of the lost souls who still supported him. But he needed victory, not only for his own stature but also to appease the Almighty whom he believed he supported via violence. Whom could he trust to carry out necessary cleansing of society? Who could successfully eliminate the pesky clergy golfers who continued to disgrace him and interfere with his plans? Claude decided that it was time to contemplate taking a more active role himself.

Max swung by Mitch's home to pick up him and Priscilla before going to gather Melody. Late afternoon thunderstorms were in the forecast, but they were not yet on the horizon. An amusement park was a good place to spend a hot, muggy Saturday. Despite being as health-conscious as they were, the group was ready to indulge in some frozen treats available from the concession stands. Some fast, breezy rides would also be welcome.

"This was a good idea, Melody," Max praised as they entered the parking lot of Thrills & Spills.

"Thanks," she said, without returning his eye contact.

"Have you thought about what ride you want to do first?"

"No. I'm easy," she replied, again looking straight ahead. It was unusual for Melody not to connect more warmly with him, but she neither looked nor sounded irritated or grumpy, so Max gave her mood no more thought for a while.

Mitch spoke up from the back seat. "I'm partial to roller coasters, so the Belly Up could be a good starting point."

"I can do without the stomach-churning rides," objected Priscilla. "The Ferris wheel is more my speed."

"On a day like this, I thought that we might concentrate on the water slides," Max offered.

"I didn't even know that they have any," said Melody.

Max could have sworn that they had both seen the announcement of their addition to the park this year. "Yes, they opened them this spring," he responded, with slight hesitation. "Did you think that we all brought our swimsuits just to go for a dip at the park beach?"

"Yes, I guess so," she replied with a glance in his direction.

Trying to keep everyone happy, they started on the Ferris wheel. For a tame ride, it was always exciting to get up so high as to be able to see for miles around. The cool breeze it afforded was also welcome. Mitch and Max then rode the Belly Up—within their foursome, at least, it was a "guy thing"—before the four of them took a cruise on the Disney-like creation, Flowing Currents. Since it was now midday, with its attendant heat, they unanimously decided that it was time for Showery Chutes.

They began on one of the shortest, tamest flumes. The water temperature was just right—refreshing, not shocking. Mitch then voted for the highest slide, and before Priscilla could even voice her objection, Melody had grabbed Mitch by the hand and pulled him in the direction of the path to the top. Max was left standing with Priscilla. He felt mildly surprised by what had just happened, but the look on Priscilla's face reflected pure shock. Her mouth hung open momentarily as she looked in the direction toward which Mitch and Melody had disappeared, then turned toward Max as he sputtered, "Well, uh, what do you want to do, Priscilla?"

Her eyes darted back and forth several times as she pulled herself together. "You know that I don't feel like scaring myself to death plummeting down any huge, twisting slide. Shall we meet them at the bottom?"

"Yes, okay," Max said, feeling somewhat dismayed himself at Melody's unexpected action. He even felt a spot of jealousy and mild irritation. "But let's take that little slide over there. I bet it comes out near the mouth of the big one."

After one tame ride, Priscilla and Max made their way to the splash pool at the bottom of the Watery Rush, but although they waited there for over twenty minutes, their companions failed to surface. The odd couple rode a pair of intermediate waterslides then headed back to the mouth of the big one for another lengthy, and fruitless, wait. It wasn't until they were exiting the bathhouse, having changed from swimsuits into clothes, that Max and Priscilla were reunited with their loved ones.

"Hi," said Mitch with a sheepish smile as he approached, exchanging glances with both Max and his girlfriend. "I bet you wondered where Melody and I were?"

"The thought crossed our minds," responded Priscilla, doing nothing to conceal her sarcasm and annoyance.

"We dashed down the Watery Rush and looked around for you for a few minutes, but we got impatient and wanted to try the other advanced slide, the Cavernous Cascade. It was great! We had to ride it again and again. The twists and turns were amazing. We were trying to spot you guys, and hoping you'd show up there, but . . . anyway, what did you two do?"

Before either Priscilla or Max had a chance to speak, Melody walked over to touch Mitch lightly on the shoulder and said simply, "I'll go change," before dashing into the women's dressing room.

The ride home from the amusement park was awkward. Melody was a trifle more talkative than she had been on the way to the park, directing feedback about her day to both Max and Mitch. Priscilla had evidently experienced chills, rather than thrills and spills, that day because the vibes emanating from her were stone cold. As for Max, he wasn't sure what to think or how to feel about the day's events. He had been feeling so close to Melody, and so trusting of their relationship, that he could not fully understand her taking off with Mitch for a couple of hours of fun and frolic. It wasn't like her, and he found it hard to believe that he could have misperceived his relationship with her. His confusion only heightened when, in the process of dropping off Melody, he spotted her aiming a clandestine wink at Mitch—and then he winked at Max.

Mitch tried nicely to engage Priscilla in conversation on the way to her place. She, for her part, replied in a civil if not friendly manner. Max could hardly wait for her to go inside and for Mitch to reenter his car.

"*What* in holy tarnation was that about, partner?" Max asked as soon as Mitch's door had closed.

"Oh, and what is it to which you refer, my friend?"

Max merely looked at Mitch through the upper parts of his eye sockets, with his face tipped downward and his facial expression saying, *You know just what I'm talking about.* Max pulled away from the curb and drove down the street.

"Well, you see, good buddy, that is quite a girlfriend you have there. Yessirree, that Melody is a special lady."

"Yes," Max responded in an expectant tone.

"And she's perceptive, opinionated, and willing to act out her plans. It must be that she likes me."

"Yes, I fear that I saw that today."

"Oh, but things today are not quite as they appeared. You see . . ." Mitch's pause made Max suspect not the worst but rather that things indeed may not have been as bad as they seemed.

"Why did you wink at me?" Max inquired.

"Just in case you were suffering, I wanted somehow to signal that things were all right."

"Suffering? *Moi*? No, I'd be glad to trade girlfriends with you. After all, you know that I don't think much of Melody, and I believe that Priscilla is just peachy."

Mitch laughed. Heartily. Too heartily to be in the process of doing Max dirty.

"Okay, that's enough beating around the bush, Mitch. What's up?"

"I believe that when you get home," began Mitch, "you will receive a comforting message of reassurance from Melody. At least, Harmony told me to tell you to expect that."

"Harmony?" It now dawned on Max: Harmony must be Melody's identical twin sister! They had finally done it: the twin switcheroo.

"That's right." Mitch read his expression and mind. "That was Harmony who rescued me from the drab clutches of Priscilla today. It seems that she split from her boyfriend about a month ago and has always found me sort of, you know, cute. She wanted to test the waters with me."

"And Melody?"

"Melody had witnessed what she perceived as tension between me and Priscilla. And she had long harbored a desire to play a sisterly trick on you, just to see if they could pull it off. Your ever-faithful girlfriend was only too willing, and mischievous, to arrange today's coup."

"So," pondered Max somewhat haltingly, "we might say that Melody used Max to mess up the mismatch between Mitch and Priscilla, perhaps to help put the shrink in the pink."

"Partner, I'm glad to hear that you now fully understand the situation. Is it safe to say that Harmony fooled you pretty convincingly?"

"It's amazing what some borrowed clothing, imitative hairstyling, and identical genes can do."

"By the way, Max, how do you think today's events are going to affect my relationship with Priscilla?" asked the psychologist naively.

Max thought briefly before summing up. "Since she is an attorney, I am sure that Priscilla will be examining the evidence closely. An indictment seems certain. As for whether or not she'll want anything to do with you again, that will be determined by the strength of her convictions."

"I hope that I get sentenced to freedom—to date Harmony."

Max and Mitch may have felt fatigued by the fun and tomfoolery of their day, but that did not stop them from heading to the golf links that Saturday evening to squeeze in nine holes when there were not yet any thunderstorms in sight. What better place was there to talk about the topsy-turvy turn of events that had occurred on their double date.

They were joined by JD, invited by Mitch via text message, for more "golf therapy." JD had spent Friday evening at the weekly meeting of Holy Help. Such gatherings had recently involved about two dozen attendees, but there were many notable absentees that night. Even his friend Mike, free on bail, had excused himself from the session, insisting that JD find his own way there. When Claude, looking uncharacteristically tense and irritable, ended the meeting shortly after it had been called to order, JD and his compatriots felt befuddled. Given this abrupt change, and the lingering conflict he felt about his affiliation with HH, JD was only too glad to receive the text message from Mitch that invited him to golf that Saturday evening.

Max and Mitch, confirmed "walking members" of the USGA, were mildly slowed by exhaustion as they made their way around the front nine of Rolling Greens. The ups and downs of a day at a water park take their toll on leg muscles. They played lackadaisically but still managed to hit far more good shots than bad.

After putting out on the last hole during dusk, weighed down by their seemingly heavier golf bags, they walked slowly toward the clubhouse while still engrossed in conversation about romance, aikido, and the glories of golf. The threesome entered the pro shop, in the back room of which Max and Mitch stored their golf clubs. Max paused to tell the clerk, Janet, that she could go home a few minutes early because he would lock up. JD was sampling putters when, soon after

Janet's departure, a gentleman carrying a lightweight maroon golf bag entered the golf shop.

Max, on his way from the storage room, heard the shop door open and close; so, he emerged saying, "We're about to close up for the night. May I help you quickly with something?"

The man was not looking at Max but, instead, reaching into his golf bag. What emerged was neither a wood nor an iron but a rifle.

JD looked up from his putting practice and, after quick recognition of both the man and the imminent danger, hurled a sleeve of golf balls across the room at Claude. The package struck him ineffectually.

"Holy shit!" exclaimed Max. There before him stood an assailant, not just any man but one well-known to him, aiming a weapon in his direction.

"B-B-Bogey!" bubbled Max with surprise and alarm.

As Claude, a.k.a. Larry Bogart, raised his .30-.30 to his shoulder and took dead aim at Max, he hesitated to pull the trigger. His racing mind could not help analyzing how this wretched golf pro had both spoiled his Holy Help ambitions and helped him play better golf, a game that he simultaneously detested and revered. This momentary freeze gave Max just enough time to react.

"Out the back!" he hollered to JD. Then timing betrayed them. Max bumped right into Mitch, who was reentering the shop after having cleaned and put his clubs away, as the first shot boomed. JD fell into Max's back, finishing the process of pushing Mitch back through the doorway.

"Run," said JD from facedown on the floor. The first trickle of blood was visible from near his left shoulder blade. Max and Mitch hurriedly stooped to grab JD, boosting and dragging him through the storage facility and into the garage in which golf carts are housed for the night. Just as a bullet slammed into the connecting door jamb as they passed it, JD hunkered down between two carts and assured the guys that he'd be safely out of sight there.

Fortunately, the garage door was still open. Mitch and Max hopped into the cart closest to the doorway, the latter in the driver's seat, and drove away. *Ping!* went a bullet off the fiberglass side of the cream-colored cart. They turned the corner around the garage door and off the line of fire from the rifle. Claude clambered into a cart and, fully familiar with its easy operation, simply stepped on the accelerator pedal and was off in pursuit. A low-speed chase was underway.

Max directed the cart across the lesson tee and out into the practice fairway. In the pale light of the emerging half-moon, Mitch was able to spot range balls that had not yet been collected for reuse the next day. Mitch leaned over several times and, missing a few times, managed to scoop up four golf balls.

"Nice weapon, Mitch," said Max sarcastically. "Do you suppose that you can throw those harder and more accurately at him than he can shoot bullets at us with his rifle?"

"I do wish that they were grenades instead of Rover Range balls," Mitch retorted.

Thwack! A bullet hit the back of the guys' cart. Steering with one hand while trying to aim the rifle with the other, the sinister minister's face held a simultaneously determined and maniacal expression. He was frustrated in several ways. First of all, his cart was gaining on that of his targets at a painfully slow pace. Secondly, unlike the bare-boned cart ahead of his, Claude's newer and costlier white version had a windshield that he was trying either to shoot around or to remove; he eventually noticed two latches that held it in place and, slowing to do so, released them. Thirdly, bouncing along over the golf balls strewn on the ground, he could not hold the rifle steady enough to fire accurately.

As the carts rumbled out of the practice area and started down the relatively smooth tenth fairway, Max veered right, heading for the series of trees in the rough that lined the hole. With the pedal to the metal, cruising at the speed of golf, he zig-zagged around some of the tree trunks, bouncing the little vehicle on protruding roots and causing bouncing Mitch to stammer, "Th-this is top speed, h-huh?" Bogey, meanwhile, stayed on the edge of the fairway, slowly gaining ground on the pursued cart because of the lighter weight he carried and the smoother, straighter path he chose. It was still a cumbersome task, but he managed to brace and steady his weapon on the move. He was just taking aim at a clearing in the trees ahead when Max executed a sharp right turn and headed across the eighteenth fairway.

Bogey bounced through the tree line and stayed in cold pursuit, squinting into the twilight darkness to keep track of his prey. Mitch pivoted in his seat to hurl a golf ball at the cart behind them, missing the vehicle that had now edged within thirty yards of theirs.

Rolling Greens was known for its undulating greens, but the entire landscape had plenty of topographical irregularities as well. Max made little turns as he traversed the fairway, hoping to throw off Bogey's aim. More importantly, he headed for the patch of rough and more trees ahead. Another bullet sharply caromed off the roof of their cart.

"Hang on, partner," Max advised Mitch as they crossed the rough, and he made a sharp left turn. Both guys leaned left to keep the top-heavy vehicle from toppling over. Bogey should have known better. Familiar with the course, he knew they were approaching an embankment that sloped away toward the brook. Fumbling to maintain control of his gun and bouncing over tree roots, however, he waited too long to start his turn. Bogey's sudden swivel to the left took his cart past its balance point. Over the embankment he went, his cart rolling twice before landing in the shallow water.

Glancing backward, Max saw with satisfaction that his maneuver had worked. He and Mitch leapt out of the cart as soon as he stopped it. They ran back to find Bogey lying face-up in the water, groggy and barely conscious. "You're over par again, my friend," said Max.

Detective Southworth apparently had no notion of buying Max and Mitch a round of drinks during their next encounter; he wanted them down at the police station that Monday afternoon, nine days after their near-brush with death. He had arrived on the scene on Saturday evening only a few minutes after the golf cart crash, having received an anonymous call (from JD) that sent him scurrying to the golf course. Now it was time for some debriefing.

"With no small thanks to you fellas, we have blown the cover off Holy Help," the detective began when Max and Mitch had been seated in the stiff wooden chairs of the sheriff's office conference room. "When I say 'we,' I mean not only our deputy sheriffs but also the state police and a host of federal agents. I asked you guys here because, given your intimate involvement in this affair, I thought you might like to hear some of the inside dope."

"Our hopes exactly," chimed in Mitch.

"First of all, their leader. The forensic psychologists and psychiatrists have not finished their analyses of this guy, Claude, or Larry Bogart, but, so far at least, your profile of him as paranoid seems to fit him like a glove. The doctors say he is 'grandiose'—that's another way of saying he has what you said, 'delusions of grandeur?'"

"Yes, that's true," confirmed Mitch.

"Yet he was modest and unassuming on the golf course," added Max.

"Well, Claude thinks that he is the greatest thing since rubber tires. When young, he was bullied by his peers because of perceived eccentricities. He apparently compensated for that because he talks like he is God's gift to humanity. Raised in a deeply religious home by hypocritical parents who frequently belittled and punished him, he came up with his own idea of God—one shaped in his own image. Furthermore, as you had predicted, he felt threatened by anyone who failed to embrace him and his religious fanaticism. We certainly knew about the high-profile murders of clergy committed by him and his henchmen. What we have recently learned is that he was also responsible for several homicides of regular, working-class guys in the Buffalo and Rochester areas during the past few years. If he recruited new members to his group and they showed anything less than complete loyalty and devotion, then he got scared and branded them as traitors to the cause."

"What a creep!" Max reacted.

"But not someone totally undeserving of pity," put in Mitch. "It sounds as though the guy was a monster who was partly made, not born."

"You may give him sympathy, or empathy, or whatever it is you psychologists have to offer," replied the duty-bound detective, "but I simply want to see him locked up, away from society for the rest of his life."

"But, Detective, how did he manage to build an organization?" Max inquired. "How many people believed in him? And how the heck did he mastermind all of those killings?"

"The guy is sharp. He is remembered as a social misfit in high school, where his only extracurricular activity was—you might guess this—the rifle club. He was an average marksman, but his grades were aces. He got into MPI, Massachusetts Polytechnic Institute, where he studied engineering and found the time to take up the game of golf. Meanwhile, he dropped into every one of the churches in the Boston area and left each one of them feeling that he had better ideas than they did. He's a religious fanatic who could not find a home. So, I guess that he just turned ugly. Maybe because he saw so many clergy and professors to imitate, or because of his own talent, he became quite good at making speeches and preaching sermons himself."

"He's a charismatic speaker?" asked Mitch for clarification.

"Yes, that's the word for him—charismatic. He was able to persuade at least two dozen guys to believe in him and his highfalutin religion. Of course, the brethren he attracted were social misfits and malcontents themselves. They were ripe for the picking, and he lured them into his cult."

Mitch wondered aloud, "I find it strange that Claude, or Bogey, was himself a golfer, yet he claimed to hate clergy members who golf. And why was he taking lessons from Max, whom he eventually tried to kill?"

"You're the psychologist," said the detective. "That's for you to figure out."

"It makes me shudder to reflect on the times I taught Bogey. I can't pretend to understand him. But I'm more curious to know about those weird guns they used," Max added. "Were they something he learned to make from his engineering background?"

"Yes, those babies were all his. Pretty impressive weapons too. When you were kids, did you guys ever have or see burp guns—you know, those plastic rifles with fat barrels? You pump air into them by pulling on a sliding handle under the barrel, and they can shoot ping pong balls fifteen or twenty feet."

"Yeah, sure," Mitch and Max agreed.

"Claude obviously wanted something much more powerful than a toy yet quieter than a firearm. Perhaps he had an air gun when he was on the high school rifle team. The most powerful such rifle that is commercially available is the spring-piston variety, not the pneumatic pump or CO^2 type. The spring-piston, that shoots BBs or pellets, is also the quietest type of air gun."

"That explains why we heard no shots," said Mitch.

"He built a heavy-duty burp gun with an aluminum barrel, gave it a sidelever-cocking spring-piston mechanism that is much larger than that of normal air guns, and had himself a deadly weapon. Together with a telescopic sight and high-compression golf ball, he and his cronies could shoot pretty accurately across long distances."

"Gee, you don't suppose. You see, I have this golf tournament coming up, and my driving accuracy hasn't been all that it should be," Max began, "but, naw, I guess not."

The detective asked, "How's that young man, JD, doing?"

Max replied, "We visited him yesterday in the hospital. He's recovering slowly from the bullet wound that had entered the right-center of his back and lodged in his rib cage without, fortunately, penetrating any vital organs. Weakened by the internal bleeding and the surgery to remove the bullet, he's been in the hospital for over a week. His discharge, however, is scheduled for the day after tomorrow." Max held his tongue about JD's confession of having known Claude personally due to his lukewarm attraction to the HH ideology. "He hopes to play golf with us again as soon as he is able."

"Speaking of golf, how were you playing that day at Rolling Greens when we were all so rudely interrupted by violence?" Mitch asked Detective Southworth.

"Wholly badly. I must have been more than thirty over par after fifteen holes, so I was sort of glad to get back to work," he admitted good-naturedly. "And speaking of getting back to work . . . Come with me, you guys. I'd like to introduce you to somebody."

The "somebody" was Captain Dillon, Commander of Troop M of the New York State Police. And he was expecting them. He awarded plaques entitled "Meritorious Service to Law Enforcement" to Max and Mitch. The lads were so surprised that they had to choke back a few tears of pride when they heard him read the word "valor" as part of the inscription.

XVI

STRAIGHT SHOOTING

EVEN THOUGH THEIR MATCH HAD NEVER BEEN COMPLETED due to villainous interruption, Rabbi Greene and Father Mulligan gladly paid off their debt by caddying for Max and Mitch. The pair did not play too well—maybe because of the clergymen's frequent throat-clearing, faux sneezing, handing them the wrong clubs, and muttering nonsensical prayers before their shots—but a good time was had by all.

Rabbi Greene said, "I have a little story to embellish this experience for you two. Three very religious rabbis in black with long beards were about to play golf. A guy named Mulrooney wanted to play a round as well, and this was the only threesome available with whom he could play. So, he joined the rabbis for eighteen holes. At the end of the game, his score was one hundred four. The rabbis shot sixty-nine, seventy, and seventy-one. Mulrooney asked them, 'How come you all play such good golf?' The lead rabbi said, 'When you live a religious life, join and attend temple, you are rewarded.' Mulrooney loved golf and figured, 'What do I have to lose?' So he found a temple close to his home, attended twice a week, converted to Judaism, joined and lived a holy life. About a year later, he again played golf with the three rabbis. Mulrooney shot one hundred while they scored sixty-nine, seventy, and seventy-one. He said, 'Okay, I've joined a temple, live a religious life, and I'm still shooting lousy.' The second rabbi inquired, 'What temple did you join?' Mulrooney said, 'Beth Shalom.' The rabbi retorted, 'Schmuck! That one's for tennis.'"

Not to be outdone, Father Mulligan decided further to distract Max and Mitch with a tale of his own. "A Catholic priest and a nun were playing a round of golf. The priest stepped up to the tee and took a mighty swing. He missed the ball entirely and cursed, 'Shit, I missed.' Sister Maureen told him to watch his language. At the next tee, Father Appleway whiffed again. 'Shit, I missed.' 'Father, I am not going to play with you if you are going to keep swearing.' The priest promised to do better. At the next tee, however, another swing and miss led to the habitual response, 'Shit, I missed.' Sister Maureen was really mad now and said, 'Father, God is going to strike you dead if you keep swearing like that.' On the following tee, the priest could not suppress the same sequence—a swing, a whiff, and 'Shit, I missed.' Out of the sky came a tremendous bolt of lightning that struck Sister Maureen dead in her tracks. The skies opened up, and a booming voice bellowed, 'Shit, I missed.'"

Both Max and Mitch mishit their subsequent approach shots to the green and three-putted, as well.

Mitch and Max decided that it was only fair to reciprocate, so they appeared together at two different Sunday schools the following morning. Their presentations may have been more secular than religious, but their message of ethics and etiquette (with funny stories aside) was recognized for its universal value. The children particularly enjoyed their question-and-answer sessions that mingled God, golf, and integrity.

The next time that Max and Mitch double-dated was an evening to remember. Max just couldn't take his eyes off Melody—and Harmony. He must have looked from one to the other two hundred times, yet remained amazed at their physical similarity. They could have been poster children for the "nature" side of the timeless nature-nurture debate. Despite their remarkable resemblance to one another, however, Max had no trouble telling them apart side-by-side. Sure, their hairstyles differed slightly, and they wore clothes that were wholly different. But, more than those superficial features, it was the look in Melody's eyes whenever her gaze met his that gave her away. Her affection for Max poured out unmistakably—and blended with the reciprocal feelings that flowed her way from him.

The happy couple were so devoted to their professions, avocations, and friends that they dared not discuss the future of their relationship in detail. Neither wished to disturb the other's lifestyle; it was what helped to make each so lovable in his or her own right. And neither wanted to upset the other by suggesting that their devotion was hampered in any way by a need for legal commitment. Their dedication to one another remained implicit. They had, however, perhaps in response to the relentless ticking of their biological clocks, decided mutually to rear a little one.

"What shall we name her?" asked Melody. Mitch and Harmony were still shaking their heads at the announcement by Max and Melody. They certainly wanted no part of responding to her request for suggestions. But Max, as he should, had a strong opinion about the matter.

"As a long-time student of aikido and fan of the martial arts, I feel philosophically and spiritually tied to the Orient. Some of the guiding principles of aikido have often been likened to those of Zen Buddhism, though Taoist philosophy—that of harmoniously balancing the forces of good and evil, of weak and strong, of *yin* and *yang*—might better capture the essence of our peaceful art of self-defense. After all, you'll recall that aikido means 'the way of harmony with nature.' Thus, I humbly submit for your consideration the name of Taog."

"Taog? Like spelled T-A-O-G but pronounced 'dowg?'" inquired Melody. Mitch began to snicker with glee. Harmony just kept shaking her head. "Hmmm. I think I like it. Yes, that's the way to go."

"Yippee! Did you hear that?" Max inquired of the young canine they had just acquired from the animal shelter. "You are a puppy on a spiritual path."

"That's the right tool for the job." JD handed Max his five-iron for his second shot on the long par-4 eighteenth hole of Holey Acres Golf Club. Max could not understand how JD had learned his golf game, and how to analyze both shots and putts, in so short a period of time. Max knew even less about how the young man was managing to cope with his long-term state of depression and getting over the shame of his having been so close to committing acts of violence on behalf of Holy Help, but Max took Mitch's word for those things. And whatever Max could not understand about JD did not matter as he started to prepare to hit that five-iron shot. Neither did it matter that he stood seven under par for thirty-five holes, leading the Northeastern U.S. Championship of Teaching Professionals. Heck, the fact that he was on the brink of qualifying for his first tour event—a major championship, no less, the PGA—had no place in his consciousness right now. Max visualized the ideal shot to the perfect target, took a deep and easy breath, and relaxed his jaw and shoulders as he addressed the ball. He saw it, felt it, and did it.

"Wisdom is knowing what to do next, skill is knowing how to do it, and virtue is doing it."

—David Starr Jordan

"Like the eye of the typhoon, which is always peaceful, inner calm results in great strength of action."

—Koichi Tohei

ACKNOWLEDGMENTS

My identity and writing have been shaped by my parents, Louis and Anne Wallace, brother, Dr. Larry Wallace, and countless teachers, friends, readings, and experiences over the years. I have the luxury of time to write thanks to the love and support of my wife and our esteemed daughters. Professor Taitetsu Unno led me into aikido, while Roderick Kobayashi Sensei and my fellow students subsequently honed my skills over the years. Specific to this book, I'm grateful for the editorial assistance of Emily Temple, Ph.D., and Megan Doyle, along with the design skills of the team at Mascot Books.

ABOUT THE AUTHOR

James Wallace, Ph.D., has spent his career practicing as a clinical psychologist, educational psychologist, and sport psychologist. He has practiced golf a lot, too, with little success. He has earned his knowledge of aikido by serving as the chief instructor (Sensei) of two dojos in Southern California and one in Ithaca, NY, before running the Colgate University Aikido Club in Hamilton, NY, the past quarter of a century. He lives there with his wife, Colgate University Professor Ann Jane Tierney, and he teaches P.E. courses in wellness, as well. They have two young adult daughters, Jasmine and Gemma, striving to live well in Virginia and Colorado, respectively. Dr. Wallace is the author of a nonfiction book about the physical and mental aspects of athletics, *On Target: Comparative Challenges of Sports & Games,* along with several magazine articles about aikido. See www.eqpsych.com and drjimswhims.home.blog for more information from Dr. Wallace, who is also available on Facebook and LinkedIn.